THE WOMEN OF MORNING

THE WOMEN OF MORNING

by
Alan Sewart

Dales Large Print Books
Long Preston, North Yorkshire,
England.

British Library Cataloguing in Publication Data.

Sewart, Alan
   The women of morning.

   A catalogue record for this book is
   available from the British Library

   ISBN 1-85389-347-1 pbk

First published in Great Britain by Robert Hale Ltd.,
1980

Copyright © 1980 by Alan Sewart

Published in Large Print 1992 by arrangement with the
copyright holder.

All rights reserved. No part of this publication may be
reproduced, stored in a retrieval system, or transmitted in any
form or by any means, electronic, mechanical, photocopying,
recording or otherwise, without the prior permission of the
Copyright owner.

LINCOLNSHIRE
COUNTY COUNCIL

Printed and bound in Great Britain by
T.J. Press (Padstow) Ltd., Cornwall, PL28 8RW.

CHAPTER 1

The woman ran away from fear—towards respite.

She ran awkwardly, clumsily. Her legs had the feeling of liquid-filled tubes about to bulge and buckle. Her chest ached from the unaccustomed strain of running and there was a rasping soreness in her throat as tides of air ebbed and flowed. Her left hand, white-knuckled, gripped the broken strap of her handbag and the bag itself swung rhythmically against her left thigh—thumping in crazy measure with every weary stride.

A hundred yards to the town's main street—no more than that—and she'd make it easily if she kept moving. Already she could see the brighter glow and she kept her eyes trained on it as she ran.

Hot-branded on her body she could still feel the stigma of the man's touch. The arm that had come frighteningly from behind her, to grip around her shoulders, crushing her breasts. The fingers of his free hand, probing, pressing into the soft flesh of her lower belly. She could still hear the ringing sound of her own screams and the guttural curse forced from her attacker's lips as she ground her heel against his shins.

Whether or not the man still followed she had no way of knowing. Impossible to look back—she couldn't bring herself to do that for anything. But she knew there would be no cessation of electrifying fear until she felt the yellow lights about her, saw the familiar shop frontages, reached the comforting sanctuary of peopled pavements.

The grey metal pedestrian-control railings barred her way, but beyond them was freedom. At other times she would have followed the railings round the curve of the pavement edge, sedately and decorously, till she reached the gap and passed through onto the pelican crossing. Now, the urgency of flight spurred her to indecorous acts. Hitching her skirt above her knees she thrust a leg through the bars, bent low, dragged the trailing leg through after her and sobbed with relief as her feet came together in contact with the friendly surface of the carriageway.

And still she kept on running.

There were lights now, of many kinds. Lights above and about her, bathing her shaking body in warm illumination. Lights that winked and alternated, changing colour and swirling shadows like some hectic outdoor discotheque. And other lights also dazzling and moving nearer. Bearing down on her.

At once, the old fear vanished in the face of a new fear. A fear of a more immediate kind that rushed up on her, belabouring her with noise.

★ ★ ★ ★

Daylight was a wind's breath away.

Held in check at the pavement's edge, the green-and-white double-decker bus chugged and vibrated in its eagerness to break the shackles of inertia.

Sitting snugly in his cab up forward, Bill Merricks turned his head to watch the rear loading door, noting with mild interest the solemn, sleepy faces of his passengers. Poor sods. If they were only half as miserable as they looked it was a poor advert for the joys of a bright morning.

But then they always seemed to look like that.

They were all regulars and Merricks recognised every face. He knew them—even though, locked in splendid isolation in his little glass box, he'd never exchanged a word with any of them during all the months he'd been driving the early buses.

The bell tinkled and Merricks pulled away.

Dwarfed by his weighty charge but dictating its progress with deft touches of his fingers, he rode sultan-like from the crest of Parkdown Hill, down the slope into awakening Cotteston. He kept his foot light on the throttle, a stroking caress that gave fuel sparingly and allowed the vehicle's own weight to supply momentum. At this point it was hard to avoid moving a shade too fast. He thundered into the Market Street length and swept grandly on towards his next official stop, three hundred yards distant.

Fifty yards short of the pedestrian-crossing at the foot of the hill, Merricks cautiously covered the brake and flicked his eyes about in active search for possible hazard. Nothing moved. The road was empty of vehicles and the immediate pavements free of people. He let the bus roll, picking up speed for the run along the flat that would continue only if he willed it—and would end when he ordered it to end. Another stage of his daily journey was closing normally, without incident.

And then the woman appeared.

Swiftly and with no kind of warning, she emerged from Warwick Street, ducked through the barrier in a flurry of skirts and without looking to right or left ran full tilt into his path.

She was panting and panicky. That much Merricks noticed in the half-second before his brain flashed messages to his hands—and then he was straining, pressing and praying as he fought the controls of the ponderous rushing monster. There might have been fifteen or twenty yards to spare, but at best it was not enough. Much as he strove with wheel and brake, the bus ate up the distance, and in the last stages of the ride he felt the bump—a soft, inconsequential ripple of resistance—transmitted to his hands from the vehicle's slowing tyres.

And then the horror and the pandemonium.

Behind him, the passengers screamed and shouted their reaction to unexplained alarm. Around him, the street which had seemed empty before, teemed with running figures coming from all directions, to converge on the scene of what Merricks knew must certainly be death. He climbed from his cab into a chattering crowd of shocked and curious people.

Merricks needed help desperately.

But there were many supporters here. Shocked or not, there would be willing helpers among the growing crowd.

'For Christ's sakes somebody get on the phone,' he shouted in a voice unrecognisable as his. 'Get the police, the ambulance.'

'I've got it, Mate. You just keep everybody back.'

Hopefully, he turned to face the speaker.

It was a constable—a young man with baby face but dressed in capable blue—and like all policemen these days he had his little radio. Merricks felt the uplift of salvation, but it was a fleeting joy. He moved alongside the bus to see at first hand the damage he had done.

The woman was not dead.

She was unconscious and mangled in the most dreadful way, but not dead. Merricks wished briefly that it were otherwise, that she had been killed outright, then reviled himself silently for the ignoble thought. While life remained there was something

12

to be salvaged. Mouthing the words, he cursed the laws of chance, realising that one more yard, one more stride, would have carried her clear, and then this heavy load of guilt would not have settled on his mind.

When Merricks reached her, the woman was lying under the vehicle midway between front and rear wheels—lower body covered, trunk and head clear. Lying there she looked normal, unmarked, but he knew there would be marks. He forced himself to bend and peer under the apron of the bus, followed with his eyes the bulky curve of her hips and the pink slope of her thighs. Only then did normality terminate in two flattened, bloody, split ribbons of flayed flesh.

After which there was nothing but the waiting.

That—and the fight to contain his foaming stomach as, grey-faced, he stood with the young constable and held the crowd at bay. It seemed an age before the first unmelodious horn split the air and the first flashing light, blue and intimidating, came tearing along the street. A red and white police car of the type contemptuously labelled a 'jam-butty' car. A car to be shunned and avoided when speed was in issue, but to be welcomed now, when shock and trouble seethed in his head.

But things were happening now.

The ambulance would be here shortly, to bear the victim away. Her future—if she had any—would then be the responsibility of someone else. But for Merricks, the weary business of explanation and self-recrimination was only just beginning.

★ ★ ★ ★

Accidents on the highway, particularly serious ones involving motor-vehicles, affect different people in very different ways.

Considered in the mass they are expressed as figures, cold and unfeeling as only figures can be. The statistics of dead and injured, annually churned out by a variety of agencies, are grim enough, yet they make dull reading for any but the dedicated preventionist.

Looked at singly, each separate accident is seen in much more human terms by those closely concerned with it—often people whose interests lie elsewhere and who can no more appreciate statistics than the finer details of horse-racing form.

14

The driver of the vehicle is often blameless, but he is always responsible. He bears the twin crosses of concern for the victim and fear of official retribution. The victim knows pain and suffering in the short term, followed rapidly by maiming or death. And if death is cheated, the later effects can be social or economic disaster of some other kind. Friends and loved-ones of the victim suffer in varying degrees according to the strength of their individual relationship with the victim, being at best distressed and at worst subjected to lasting anguish.

Policemen, ambulance-men and others whose task it is to pick up the pieces are *prima facie* a pretty thick-skinned breed, prepared to examine, process and report the most hideous calamities with apparent calm. They are, of course, neither calm nor callous. They are simply inured to the unpleasant—overtly unresponsive to the sufferings of others. They have built around themselves a shield of contrived indifference which cloaks their true feelings —a shield without which they would never be able to operate as effectively as they do.

Bill Merricks, ashen faced, trembly and

upset, co-operated as well as he could with P.C Ron Fairclough the first policeman on the scene and with P.Cs Kevin Nelson and Jim Forbes of Headquarters, Traffic Branch, who took over the reporting of the matter. The two traffic men were proficient at First Aid, but mercifully in the present case such ministrations were unnecessary. They would, in any event, have been limited in scope.

The patient was removed by ambulance to the Cotteston Royal Infirmary and afterwards Nelson and Forbes busied themselves with those other duties which, over many years of service, they had come to regard as routine.

They controlled traffic, took measurements, noted details, interviewed witnesses, checked documents and inscribed ticks in the squares and columns of accident reporting books. Remarkably quickly after the event they arranged for the removal of the bus, and when that was done the flow of early morning traffic through the town continued uninterrupted.

Forbes made careful note of a point that arose from his interview with the driver.

'She looked scared to hell about something,' Merricks said.

'So would you be, Mate, with a flaming great bus on top of you,' Forbes said, tartly.

'No. I mean before that. Before she saw the bus.'

'You mean she was running away from something else?'

'That's the way it looked to me.'

Forbes digested the information.

'We'll have to ask her about it,' he said, 'but we can't do much before. And if I'm any judge it'll be a good few days before that girl's well enough to be interviewed.'

CHAPTER 2

Jenny Collinge was only half awake.

Her golden hair was tangly and pillow-mussed and her cheeks were stained with traces of yesterday's eye shadow. Her lips pouted, innocent of their normal shaping of mauve lipstick and her eyes lacked sparkle under their heavy lids. No breakfast had sustained her—not even so small a comfort as a reviving cup of tea—and the peeping circle of early morning sun crept upwards faster than her spirits.

She'd fallen for it again.

She was heading for work in an all-fired hurry, more than an hour in advance of the start of her normal shift. This wasn't the first time it had happened and it was getting a bit thick. Just because she was a woman. Things like this never seemed to appear in the reckoning when silly people talked about the easy life a woman police constable led.

Woman Police Constable!

God, what a ridiculous title. *Policewoman* had always seemed so much better, more ladylike. But then 'Miss' was so much nicer than this 'Ms' thing that was trying to be popular and one was part and parcel of the other.

Hunched in the back seat of the little Ford, she glanced glumly at her wristwatch and tightened her lips against the rumblings of rebellion in her heart. Most times when they sprang this hurry-up job on her she didn't mind—she even found it quite exciting—but last night had been a particularly heavy night and Jenny had been looking forward to a reasonable quota of sleep.

Still, it had been a good night too. A

18

minor triumph.

For weeks past she'd been angling away, trying to inveigle that nice Laurie Flood into asking her out. And last night she'd finally managed it.

He'd turned out to be a good dancer as well as excellent company, fairly well blessed with funds and quite generous in the way he'd spent. On the debit side though, he'd hit the bottle a bit too heavy and tried to persuade Jenny to do the same. And later, when he'd dropped her off at her lodgings at some ungodly hour of the morning she'd had to watch out for his roving hands.

But that was all right as long as she kept it in check. A girl could cope with a certain amount of male ambition—could almost feel flattered by it—and in the end, that was what life was all about.

Life was about something else today, though.

Considering present realities, Jenny's life seemed to be all about getting called out early and having to chase off to work, unwashed, unfed and feeling like a rag-bag. What in heaven's name was bugging Sergeant Toban this time, she wondered? P.C Dick Potter who'd rattled gravel against her window, urged her to dress and turn out, and was now steering the juddering little panda car towards Cotteston Central Police Station, hadn't been much help. He'd been able to tell her next to nothing about the job—except that it was about a handbag.

A handbag snatch.

A simple little case of theft, just like dozens of other little crimes that happened every day in the wide, sprawling and cosmopolitan New Town of Cotteston. The place was known to be full of thieves—generations of thieves including the very old, the brash beginners and every shade and sort in between. So what was Sergeant Toban so het-up about? Potter had told her it was urgent, but if a simple handbag snatch was the urgent matter involved, it was far too tiny a thing in Jenny's view to justify turning out a woman police constable so early in the morning.

The whole thing sounded rather like panic-stations.

Jenny could understand some of the younger, less experienced sergeants going haywire about something and nothing. But not Toban. Sergeant Toban was an able supervisor who handled all aspects of police work with the greatest skill and confidence. He probably knew more about interviewing women than Jenny did herself. Yet he had sent for her to help out with what sounded like a very minor matter.

That was a dubious fact. Unlikely though it seemed, the incident must have proved in some way too much for Toban.

Riding in through the awakening town centre, Jenny composed herself as best she could, smoothing out her wrinkled nylons, twisting the slim blue uniform skirt into line and fussing with the hastily donned black bow tie. Appearances mattered very much to her and it was a matter of pride that she should arrive to face the problem—whatever it turned out to be—without seeming to be a tired young lady, freshly dragged from sleep.

The uniform neatened, she took a handkerchief and a vanity case from her shoulder-bag and used the dying moments of the ride to repair the ravages a shortened night had worked on her pretty face.

Sergeant Toban was waiting in the front office.

There was a sombre frown on his face, but he cheered visibly when he saw Jenny.

She had always had a soft spot for Geoff Toban. She liked him as a person and respected him as a superior. Much as she doubted the need for his summons she flashed him a smile of greeting, contriving to appear a good deal brighter than she felt.

'Good morning, Sergeant. What's the matter?'

He returned her smile briefly before the grave look returned to his face. He nodded towards the interview room.

'You'd better find out, Jenny my girl. That's what you're here for. We've a customer in yonder and there's something about her that puzzles me a lot.'

'It's just a bag snatch, isn't it?' she questioned. 'That's what Dick Potter says anyway.'

He nodded.

'On the face of things, yes. But there's something more than that, I can tell by the way she's acting-up. I've done the best I can, but she isn't prepared to discuss it with me.' He grinned ruefully. 'I've always reckoned to be able to get women talking, but I can make no progress at all with that one.'

'What sort of mood is she in?'

'A bit angry and a bit frightened. We've had her here for more than an hour already and she isn't very happy about it. That's why I decided to turn you out early. Sorry I've had to drag you out, Jenny, but I'm hoping she'll talk to you.'

'What about filling in a few details? I've got nothing so far.'

'Fair enough, but it'll sound pretty common stuff, just like it sounded to me. She was waiting at a bus stop in Halcombe Road when some yob came along and grabbed her handbag. I got that out of her without any trouble, but then she clammed up and came all over secret. As soon as I started trying to dig, she calmly announced that she'd only talk about it to a woman. Now that might mean very little or it might mean a hell of a lot, but whatever it is I can't let her go till I've bottomed it, one way or the other.'

'How do you want it handled?'

'Just go in there and smooth her down. Then find out what it is that's bothering her. We can't do a damned thing about it till we know. I'm relying on you, Jenny.'

Jenny turned to tackle the impending interview and the weight of weariness seemed to slip away from her shoulders. So they were relying on her, were they? Just as men always had to rely on women when this kind of problem came along. Most of the time, Jenny felt a bit of a poor relation amongst her male colleagues who were older, wiser, stronger than she. But sometimes the special advantages a woman had were seen in their proper light—and this was such an occasion.

'I'll give it a spin, Sarge,' she said.

★ ★ ★ ★

The woman was old enough to be Jenny's mother. Well—a young mother, anyway.

She was perhaps fortyish. Age apart though, she had the look of a spinster, butter-mouthed and prim, hair mousing a bit, clothes dowdy and unfashionable, face clean but unmade-up, eyes red and puffy with crying.

She was sitting on a hard chair and twisting a handkerchief between her fingers—fingers that were innocent of rings, Jenny noticed.

When Jenny entered the room the woman looked up expectantly and her eyes brightened in obvious relief. Jenny

24

smiled at the woman and picked up in return all the flashed messages of distress. No liberated brazen this. Some women had little modesty these days and were brash enough to talk about the most intimate things to the first friendly face, whether it be male or female. But a few were old-fashioned enough to fight very shy of men whenever they were in some kind of trouble. This red-faced, helpless creature was clearly one of the latter breed.

Recognising all the signs, Jenny saw at once that there had been wisdom in Toban's decision to call her out.

But whatever was on the woman's mind, she'd talk now. It was only a question of deciding how best to begin.

There were several hard-backed chairs in the small room, positioned austerely round a scrubbed white-wood table. Choosing a chair, Jenny sat down facing the woman, smoothed her skirt and tried to look encouraging.

'What's the matter, love?' she began. 'Somebody stole your handbag, did they?'

'That's right. At the bus stop.'

'How much is missing?'

'Nothing.'

'Nothing?' Jenny was puzzled and it

showed on her face. 'Then I don't understand...'

But the woman was beginning to unfreeze and words bubbled from her lips.

'Bless you, dear,' she said. 'I'm not worried about an old handbag. Besides, the policeman got it back for me—found it just round the corner, thrown over a wall into somebody's garden. There wasn't much money in it, anyway, just a few pounds, and when the policeman found the bag the money was still there. Every bit of it. No, dear. It's not the handbag I'm worried about.'

So Sergeant Toban had been quite right. There *was* some other thing, and it seemed to Jenny that a revelation was about to be made.

'What, then?' she prodded.

'It was the way he took it.'

The woman leaned forward in her chair and gave Jenny a conspiratorial look—a woman's look to another woman.

'He felt me all over.' She touched her body in various places. 'Here, here and here. He frightened me half to death, the brute.'

So that was the way of it.

In a technical sense it was an indecent assault, though not a particularly serious one, and as such the complaint was a crushing anticlimax. Jenny was surprised to find it was no more than that, and disappointed too, in a perversely unprofessional way. There must be very few women, she reasoned, who would have been even the tiniest bit too embarrassed to mention that kind of assault to an obvious father-figure such as Sergeant Toban.

The drab little woman was extra-timorous, prudish almost, which was well out of the ordinary in these permissive days. Why, only a few hours earlier, Jenny herself had had to repulse Laurie Flood in the same...

But that was an entirely different circumstance and she brushed aside the associated thought. The woman was entitled to her fit of squeamishness—entitled to have her complaint investigated according to the law.

Jenny knew what was wanted now.

Reaching into a sectioned cabinet standing against the wall she took out a sheet or two of plain paper.

'Don't worry,' she told the woman. 'We'll sort this out for you in a jiffy. Now

I want you to tell me everything you can remember about what happened. I'll only scribble a few notes to begin with, and when you're sure you've told me everything I'll take down a proper statement.'

★ ★ ★ ★

Afterwards, it was Toban's turn to be surprised.

'There, but for the grace of God...' he chuckled. 'When I was a few years younger, Jenny... But enough of that. Half of it's not fit for your tender ears.'

'You want me to go ahead with it, Sarge?'

He checked his watch and whistled silently.

'Oh yes, it'll need to go in, Jenny. But let's play it nice and easy. The C.I.D lads should be in any time now. I think you should see Sergeant Hollis and find out what he has to say about it.'

★ ★ ★ ★

Detective Sergeant Matt Hollis read the statement through, fingered his crinkly ginger hair and frowned in thought.

28

'It's all about the indecency bit, Jenny,' he said. 'That's what's bugging her—not having her handbag nicked.'

'She felt violated, Sarge, not robbed.'

He pricked his ears up at her last word.

'Why do you say that? There's no suggestion of robbery, is there?'

'No. At least... I'm not sure.'

'But you took the statement, Jenny, and I've read it. She isn't complaining of robbery, is she? He pinched her bag, then put his arms round her and fondled her. That's her word—not mine. He *fondled* her.'

'That's right, Sarge.'

'There's no suggestion that he used force on her *in order to steal?*'

'Nothing like that. Not from what she said.'

'And he already had the bag when he did the fondling bit?'

'That's right.'

'O.K So that gets robbery out of the way. I wanted to be quite sure about that. Well then, we're left with one theft and one indecent assault.'

'Yes. That's the way she described it.'

He tossed the statement onto his

blotting-pad, leaned back in his chair and smiled at Jenny Collinge.

'It sounds a bit thin to me, Jenny.'

'But it's the truth, Sarge. I'd swear to it.'

'Oh, I'm not saying I disbelieve the story, because I don't.' He spoke slowly, patiently, explaining facts to a junior colleague. 'The point is, it won't be easy to prove. She had her handbag pinched all right—that's not disputed. We've got the bag back and with any luck there'll be prints on it, so that part shouldn't be difficult. The indecency, though. That's different. On what we've got so far it would never stand up in court against a crafty defence solicitor, and we've got our share of those. I can see a guilty plea to theft and a strong denial of the rest. And where would that get us?'

Jenny coloured, but it was a flush of anger, not embarrassment.

'He didn't have to put his hands where he put them,' she said hotly. 'He didn't have to do a survey to find out what her body was like.'

He grinned and nodded.

'All right. Nobody would quarrel with that. But show me the evidence. To begin with, there aren't any witnesses, so it's him against her. The woman's own statement hinders rather than helps if you think about it. He fondled her—so she isn't bruised or scratched—and her clothing isn't torn. All we have is a woman who says a man touched her in the wrong places. Where do we go for corroboration, Jenny?'

'She complained about it straight away.'

'That's exactly what she *didn't* do. I'd be a lot happier if we had a decent 'fresh complaint' statement. But this woman worked against herself. She said nothing about indecency at the time, and then she sat in the station for a couple of hours before she mentioned it at all.'

'Only because she didn't like mentioning it to a man.'

'We know that, Jenny, but she's a grown woman, not a little girl. The fact that she coughed it out as soon as she saw another woman might help a bit, but not much in my opinion. The court would have to rule on that one. Look at it from the defence point of view. They'd say she sat in the nick for two hours concocting a story to get their client in trouble, and the court would probably rule against her. If that happened, we'd never prove our case. The defence would have an easy time of it. They only have to raise a doubt in the court's mind and they're entitled to the benefit of that doubt. If they admitted touching at all—which I doubt—they'd say it was accidentally done in the course of theft and there was no indecency in the man's mind or in the circumstances.'

But Jenny was unconvinced.

'Why should he touch her at all, Sarge? He was standing right next to her at the bus stop. He took hold of her handbag and snatched it from her. Why didn't he just run away if he only wanted the handbag?'

'Well, we both know the answer to that one, Jenny. But knowing it's one thing—proving it's another.'

'And there's something else,' Jenny went on. 'He obviously didn't want the bag or he wouldn't have thrown it away. I think that proves he wanted something else.'

'It might only prove he got cold feet.'

'Are you saying he couldn't ever be charged with the assault, Sarge?'

'No, I'm not saying that. If we got a bit more evidence, that might give us a stronger case.'

'How could we get more evidence?'

'It's hard to say, Jenny. But suppose when we catch the bloke he decides to admit it. In that case, he'll certainly be charged.'

She pouted in disappointment.

'I think you're on his side,' she said.

Matt Hollis grinned widely.

'Stop fighting me, Jenny, for God's sake. I agree with what you say. I believe the old dear *was* indecently assaulted and I'm quite sure this wasn't just a handbag snatch.'

'That isn't the way it sounds, Sarge. Everything I've said so far, you've argued against. You sound very sceptical to me.'

'But I'm not, Jenny. I'm just weighing up the merits of the case, that's all. I'm convinced your complainant's telling the truth. She has to be. It fits the pattern.'

'The pattern?' Jenny was as surprised as she sounded. Matt Hollis widened his grin.

'That's right, the pattern. This is the second job of the same type. The first one was two days ago—a young woman waiting for an early bus at a stop in King Street. The chap came up behind her and snatched her handbag. I spoke to the woman myself and she said she thought his hands strayed more than they needed to.'

'I hadn't heard about that one.'

'Probably not. We crimed it as a straight theft.'

'but if it was an indecent assault...'

This time, when he replied, he sounded a little weary.

'You're missing the point, Jenny. The crime was reported to us as a straight theft. What the complainant said about the thief having adventurous hands was just a little comment on the side that made me prick my ears up. She was mentioning it, not complaining about it. She certainly didn't make as much of it as this other woman does.'

'You're saying not to bother with this latest one, aren't you?'

'Nothing of the sort. In fact I'm very interested in this one, because it turns a nothing into a something.'

'I don't get you.'

'Well, the first one was no more than a hint, Jenny. It might have been sheer accident. But with this latest job coming along it looks as though there was more to the first than I thought. Same time, same M.O It looks as though we've got a crank started up in business.'

'All right then. What do you want me to do about it?'

'The latest case? Crime it, Jenny. Put it through as theft from the person. Let's have that description of the man circulated and we'll get the lads busy trying to find him.'

'And the statement?'

'Send it in with the file. Include the details as part of the story. In the meantime I'll see the word gets round and we can start keeping an eye on all these unattached females who seem to be standing at our bus stops in the early morning.'

CHAPTER 3

The amount of disquiet engendered by the incident was understandably small.

It was the first small crime of the day, and like all other small crimes it would be enquired into and the sparse leads followed. The police would crack it if they could, but if nothing in the way of more positive evidence was found it would be added to the list of offences reported—an ever lengthening list which would provide the major part of the town's criminal statistics for the year.

In common with detectives the world over, Matt Hollis had too many such bread-and-butter jobs to handle himself, and at the morning conference which took place that day and every day in the detective office at Cotteston Central Police Station, he allocated it along with other small matters to various members of his team.

Detective Constable Jack Reade was the recipient, and in handing it over, Matt had a few words with Reade.

'There's a possible link with this one, Jack. Check the crime register for the last few days.'

'You mean the King Street job, Sarge?'

'That's the one. You'll find the M.Os much the same. A suspicion of tit-stroking and the handbag thrown away round the nearest corner. Nothing missing.'

Reade compared the two cases on paper, which was as far as he could go. The similarity between them was striking but inconclusive. Afterwards he assisted Jenny to knock out the forms, circulated a message locally and arranged for the handbag to be dusted for fingerprints. He also jollied the complainant through the messy business of having her own fingers rolled in ink, explaining as a matter of course that once they'd been compared with any marks found on the handbag they would be destroyed.

The elimination prints were submitted to Headquarters along with the handbag, after which Reade busied himself with other crimes outstanding in his workload and Jenny resumed normal patrol.

For the time being, the enquiry ended there.

But police officers are earnest students of events and when—two mornings later—there was a similar theft at a bus stop some two miles from the first, Sergeant Toban spoke personally to the new complainant. She was a young student nurse, angry about the loss of her property but otherwise unflustered. She seemed surprised at some of Toban's questions.

'Did the chap touch you at all?'

'Touch me?'

'Yes, touch you.'

'Well, he was standing behind me like I told you. He reached his arm round me to grab the bag.'

'But did he touch you? You know what I mean, Miss. Did he stroke you or behave improperly?'

'He didn't get the chance, I ducked out straight away. He got the bag though,' she added ruefully, 'and all my holiday money. Where am I going to find another thirty quid?'

'Did you get the impression that he was trying to touch you?' Toban persisted.

She looked at him through narrowed eyes.

'You kinky or something, Sergeant? What's this fixation about touching?'

Toban grinned broadly and helped himself to an eyeful of her young figure. If she wanted to know, he didn't mind having the odd touch here and there, and this one would do for starters. But he couldn't tell her that.

'I'm as normal as they come, Miss, you can rest assured. No, we've had a run lately of handbag snatches with sexual overtones if you know what I mean. I'm just trying to find out if this was the same pattern.'

'Oh,' she said, still doubtful. 'Well it wasn't like that at all. He was after my

38

money, I tell you. He took my handbag, didn't he?'

And Toban admitted the justice of her words.

This time, for once, the attacker had *not* thrown the handbag away—or if he had, they hadn't found it.

★ ★ ★ ★

There were two further cases within the week.

Warming now to the trend of events, the early-morning staff were on the watch for his new sex angle and each of the complainants was discreetly quizzed.

The first, a canteen supervisor, was adamant that nothing even faintly indecent had occurred, but the officer who interviewed her got the impression that she was lying—out of embarrassment, he thought. She was also relieved to know that her property had been recovered and would be returned to her in due course and that might have made her less anxious to press the matter. Unsatisfied, the officer arranged for a woman police sergeant to interview the complainant, but she maintained her story that the incident had been theft and nothing more.

The second complainant took an opposite line.

She complained from the outset of indecent assault, in somewhat more flagrant circumstances than the others. At first she made no mention of an attempt at theft, but when questioned she recalled that the man had made a half-hearted grab at her handbag which failed.

★ ★ ★ ★

When all these reports were considered together, the C.I.D were satisfied that a more serious pattern was beginning to show. At a conference held in his office after the fifth linked case, Detective Inspector Jim Wilson went through the meagre details of available evidence.

'We've got some prints outstanding from the King Street job and the Halcombe Road job,' he said, 'and the buggers are linked. Whoever did one, did both.'

'But I understand the bloke's not on record?' Sergeant Hollis said.

'No. That's the problem, Matt. But at least it seems we can stitch him—if we can catch him.'

'What about the Market Street job, sir?'

'Nothing there. We got the bag back, but it was one of those silly things on a silver chain. It looks as though he never handled the bag itself at all.'

'But it's got to be the same bloke,' Detective Sergeant Vic Parsons said.

'Undoubtedly, Vic, and he's bang at it. Whoever this bloke is, lads, he's a sex nut of some sort. I'm as sure as I can be that pinching handbags has very little to do with what he's really after.'

'We've a bag outstanding, sir,' Parsons reminded him. 'The young nurse. The Priory Lane job.'

'I know that, Vic. It seems out of character. But we might have another look for that one. Ten to one he's stuffed it down a manhole or something. It doesn't alter my view in any way. This bugger's after sex.'

'He isn't getting much out of it, then,' Hollis said. 'So far the biggest thrill he's had is a hand up somebody's skirt. He's going to a lot of risk for a quick feel.'

'That's only so far,' Wilson said. 'But these things have a nasty habit of growing, Matt, as you know. He's found a pattern that suits him and he isn't going to pack it in as long as it keeps working. He'll get bolder and better as he goes along and we'll finish up with a rape if we aren't careful. So I reckon it's time we started being careful.'

'Want me to fix up some obboes, sir?' Hollis asked.

'Not yet, Matt. Not fixed obboes anyway. These jobs are happening at bus stops and we must have hundreds to pick from all over the town. Some early patrols might do it, laid on specially for the purpose. We know the timing and we know what to look for. They can prowl along all the main routes and keep their eyes open for possible victims.'

'Isn't there something queer about the timing?' Parsons said thoughtfully. 'Of the five cases we've had, two were just on six o'clock in the morning, one at half past six and the other two at around quarter to seven.'

'It shows a good pattern,' Wilson said.

'There's that, sir. But doesn't it show something else? What sort of crank do you suppose is out operating at that time? I've known a lot of sex-merchants in my day, but offhand I can't recall one that worked in the early morning. I'd say most blokes would find it too chilly at that hour to be getting urges.'

'And what about the women?' Jack Reade put in.

'What about 'em?' Wilson countered.

'Well, what are *they* doing out in the small hours?'

Wilson grinned knowingly.

'That's easy Jack. I've been noticing the early birds ever since I was a beat-bobby. And so have you, if you think about it. The trouble with you young sprigs is that you only start thinking about women after the sun comes up. But they're about long before that. You just watch the bus stops any day—in any town—and when most folks are still asleep you'll find women up and about. I mean women on their own, all over the place, and they're not all old hens either. You can see some nifty pieces around if you keep your eyes open.'

'I'd better start looking then,' Reade grinned. 'But why are they out, sir? Husbands kicked 'em out of bed?'

'They're earning an honest living, most of them. You might find a few old bags working late and the odd party piece who's been out all night, but most of them are just hard-working girls. They're office-cleaners, early-post sorters, nurses, shift-workers, that sort of thing. A surprising number of women go to work early.'

'And it looks as though our friend's rumbled it, whoever he is,' Matt Hollis said.

'That's how it looks, Matt. Well, we're paid to look for buggers like that, right round the clock, so if we've got an early riser, we'd better get up before he does.'

CHAPTER 4

P.C Jim Forbes had a healthy dislike of hospitals.

He'd never had to attend one as a patient and hoped he never would, but he'd seen the inside of more than a few, and to Forbes they were all depressing places.

The nurses and medical staff were always helpful and friendly, the inmates morose or cheerful according to their condition and the surroundings clinically clean. But there were always odours—not unpleasant smells, to be fair, but smells that faintly suggested carefully cloaked disease. Also there was human misery. Staff and patients alike did their best to disguise the presence of it, but Forbes knew it was there in tidy parcels on every bed.

Following the trim, blue-uniformed charge nurse through the bowels of Cotteston Royal Infirmary, Forbes steeled himself to look comfortable. He followed her into Clay Ward with a detached smile on his face, striving to avoid wrinkling his nose.

The patient he'd come to see lay isolated in a curtained bed at the far end of the ward. On his way there, he tried to avoid staring at the occupants of other beds, but they were all staring at him, all picking their small boredom-chasing thrills from sight of a policeman in uniform right there inside the ward. Forbes could feel their eyes on him and it made him uneasy. It was with a sense of relief that he ducked under the curtains behind the charge nurse to stand pink-faced beside the bed that contained the victim of his latest traffic accident case.

She was conscious, and apart from the blanket-covered cage over her lower body she seemed ordinary. But Forbes knew she was not ordinary. The Ward Sister had briefed him in advance and he knew there was little or nothing left under that innocent looking mound. Both legs amputated. Twin stumps the only legacy of a dreadful brush with a massive motorbus. It was important not to let his knowledge show, not to upset the woman by glancing too obviously towards the covered area. He fixed his eyes on her face, doffed his flat cap and grinned cheerfully.

'Hello, Mrs Gray. My name's Forbes. I've come to see you about the accident.'

'Yes. They told me you were coming.'

'I'll need to ask you some questions about what happened. Is that all right?'

The woman's face clouded and her lower lip trembled. Had his approach been too blunt, Forbes wondered? He strove to put her at ease.

'You needn't talk now if you don't feel up to it,' he said. 'Only the hospital told us you were feeling better and I thought this would be a good time. Would you rather I left it for another day or two?'

'Oh no, please. I'm feeling all right.'

'That's fine then. But look here, Mrs Gray. You can stop me if you want to, any time. Believe me, there's no hurry.' He waited for some dissent and when none came he went on, 'You remember what happened that morning?'

'Yes. I remember.'

The lip was quivering again. He waited till it settled.

'What were you doing just before it happened?'

'I was running.'

Forbes nodded and smiled encouragingly.

'The bus driver told us you were running. Why? Were you late for work or something?'

'No. I was running away. A man had just attacked me.'

★ ★ ★ ★

Forbes asked a few more questions.

The answers surprised and alarmed him. When he added their purport to what he already knew he grew less and less happy to continue the interview, more and more convinced that this was a job for another woman. He stammered his excuses, left the ward and joined P.C Kevin Nelson,

47

waiting in the police car in the Infirmary car-park.

He got through on the radio straight away.

Ten minutes later, Jenny Collinge found herself at Mrs Gray's bedside obtaining a detailed statement and one hour after that she handed the handwritten sheets directly to the man who, above all, would be interested in their contents.

★ ★ ★ ★

The conference in Detective Inspector Wilson's office was drawing to a close when Jenny entered and handed him the statement. He read it carefully, then exploded.

'Look at that bastard,' he said, passing the papers to Matt Hollis. 'Read it out, Matt, nice and loud, so we'll all know what the bugger's done this time.'

Hollis did as he was bidden.

'It's our friend the handbag man all right,' he said.

'Without a doubt,' Wilson boomed. 'And once again he had something on his mind other than handbags. Only this time, even he couldn't have imagined what it would lead to. So we've got a poor woman crippled for life. He obviously scared her out of her wits.'

'I'm not surprised,' Hollis said. 'I know that stop in Warwick Street. It's just before the railway viaduct and there are no houses just there. This grass bank she mentions, where he threw her down, is a bit of rough land near the main arch. Nobody would have seen them there. It's a good job she managed to get away.'

'I doubt if she's feeling all that lucky now,' Wilson said sombrely. 'But the point is, he had her down. The poor woman must have thought she was about to be raped. No wonder she ran. I told you this bastard would get ambitious. Now he's proved it.'

'But that must have been only his second effort, sir,' Matt Hollis pointed out. 'Look at the date. The King Street job was just the day before, only we didn't twig the implications of that one till the spinster was attacked, in Halcombe Road. The Halcombe Road job must have been number three. This one was number two.'

'That's right, Matt,' Wilson agreed, 'and since then we've had three more reported, making six in all. But this one's far and away the worst. When we get our hands on this bugger it would be nice to charge him with wounding, but I know we'd never prove intent.'

'Wait a minute, sir,' D.C Jack Reade put in. 'Hasn't there been a case on this? Something about a man who scared his wife with threats until she jumped out of a window and broke her leg? They charged him "wounding with intent".'

Reade was the acknowledged swot of the department. Wilson gazed at him with twinkling eyes.

'Keep it up, Jack, lad,' he said. 'You'll make a lawyer yet. But *R. v Chapin* happened nearly seventy years ago and I doubt if it was on all fours. In Chapin's case they had proximity. He was standing right next to her, threatening her, when she jumped. This Gray woman now, she'd run about five hundred yards before she met the bus and by then the attacker would be as far away again, in the opposite direction. Much as I hate the bastard for what happened, I can't make out that kind of case. No, lad. We've an attempted theft, an indecent assault and—if he gives us the right answers—an assault with intent to ravish at the outside. I can't see any court imputing an intent to drive the wretched woman into running under a bus.'

'But that's what she *did* do,' Reade said stubbornly.

'Quite right, Jack. And what we have to do is try to stop it happening again.'

He turned to Matt Hollis.

'Get somebody up to Warwick Street, Matt, to run the rule over that grass bank. I know it's nearly a week old, but you never know. There might be something. Oh, and lay those early patrols on. Draw up some shifts. Use our own lads, the Crime-patrols, Dog-handlers and anybody else you can slot in. These jobs could easily get bigger yet.

'I'm starting to feel uneasy.'

CHAPTER 5

It was a fine, chill morning.

The air was untainted yet with traffic fumes and Colin Duffy breathed the sweetness of it as he walked homeward along the empty street.

Another night shift over.

Nice to think that he'd finished his labours when most other people were only starting theirs. There were a few lighted windows in adjoining houses and soon there'd be more as his neighbours began to stir, but his own house was wrapped in darkness.

He halted on the doorstep and looked up at the lightening sky before keying the lock and letting himself into the gloomy hall. The warmth of the house felt comforting after the nippy air outside. Switching lights on in sequence he made his way through to the kitchen, topped up the kettle, plugged in and listened to the hum of heating water as he spooned coffee and sugar into a stained mug.

He did these things automatically, fixing his usual snack and brew before retiring. Fumbling on the pantry shelf he located the plastic biscuit-barrel and from the shallow layer of bits selected three ginger-nuts and a marshmallow. He munched noisily as he waited for the kettle to boil. The wall-clock told him it was fifteen minutes after seven. Another quarter of an hour and he'd be in bed, tucked up nice and cosy alongside Della.

Sweet Della!

When steam jetted from the kettle spout he switched off, poured and tipped milk direct from the bottle into the hot mug. He swallowed the last crumbs of the biscuits, took a cautious sip from the mug and then climbed the stairs and went into the front bedroom. Della was sleeping, but she stirred lazily when the light came on.

'That you, Col?' she mumbled.

'Who was you expecting?'

It was the oldest joke in their domestic repertoire but as always he grinned at his own remark. Della was less amused. She grunted and rolled onto her side, away from him.

'Put that damned light out and come to bed.'

He stripped quickly, scattering items about the bedroom floor. The worn tweed jacket fell first, then the blue uniform trousers, heavy boots, grey socks, shirt and underpants. He slipped into his striped pyjamas, unclipped his wristwatch, wound it and laid it on the rickety table beside the bed.

'You want a swig, Della?' he asked, offering the mug.

'No, ta.'

He always offered and Della always

declined, but he knew she'd be upset if he didn't offer. Ah well. It was a harmless foible. He finished off the sweet dregs, reached to pull the lazy-man switch and then rolled between the sheets, nuzzling up to her in the dark.

A warm bed. A warm woman.

Duffy waited a few seconds and then reached out for her. She turned her face to receive his preliminary peck and then pulled away, duty done.

'Come on, hon,' he cajoled, pulling at her arm.

'Your feet are cold as ice, Col.'

It was a familiar grumble, but it irritated him.

'Yours 'ud be bloody cold if you'd been walking fences all night,' he sulked. 'They'll soon warm up.'

He planted the offending feet on her warm buttocks and she squealed, knocking them away.

'Leave me alone, Col. I'm sleepy.'

'I'm randy,' he rejoined.

'You're always randy, Col. Go to sleep.'

Duffy frowned to himself in the darkness. He could read the signs plain enough. The bitch was going to put him off again, for the umpteenth time. It wasn't good enough—not by bloody half—but reproaches would only make her snappy and even less co-operative. He made one last persuasive effort, reaching round her plump body and stroking a warm, silk-covered breast.

'Five minutes, love. That's all.'

She pushed his hand away impatiently.

'Oh get off, Col. You're always the same.'

'You're always the bloody same too, Della,' he accused, nursing his frustration. 'Morning after bloody morning. There's never nothing doing these days.'

She twisted head and shoulders and hissed into his ear.

'You know how I feel, Colin Duffy. What sort of time's this for canoodling? It's morning. I'll be having to get up in a minute to sort the kids out ready for school. Night time, that's much better. See me tonight.'

'But I'm at work again tonight. You know that.'

'All right then—weekend. See me at weekend.'

'You're just putting me off, Della,' he said bitterly. 'As I remember, you get headaches at weekend, or the bloody rags are on or something. When the hell do I get my share?'

She yawned noisily and settled to snooze.

'You'll be all right this weekend, Col. It's a promise.'

★ ★ ★ ★

Della was snoring softly inside a few minutes, but it took Duffy half an hour to get to sleep—thirty minutes in which he cursed himself silently for not having the guts to be master in his own house.

When she was in the right mood, Della was good stuff—the best—but this night work made everything so bloody topsy-turvy. He could never catch her in the right mood so early in the day. A dozen times on the trot she'd spurned him and each time it happened—or didn't happen—he felt more thwarted and aggrieved.

One of these days he'd give it her whether she wanted it or not. That would be a new slant, guaranteed to make Della see how mad she was making him. A short, sharp, blood-and-guts rape of his own wife. It might turn out to be the very thing she needed.

In the warm silence of the bed with her body only inches out of contact, he began as usual to wallow in self-justification. He wasn't the first bloke to go hunting for what he couldn't get often enough at home. He wondered if Della realised that by depriving him as she kept doing, she was driving him off to search for somebody else. One of these days he'd fix himself up with a regular bit of fresh—somebody who wouldn't grumble and pull away whenever he felt like having his oats. Della wouldn't like it, but it was her own bloody fault, so serve the bitch right.

Only it wasn't proving all that easy.

Years before, as a single man without ties, he'd enjoyed open season on every spare piece in town. It had been easier then. Now, with a wife and kids in tow, he felt the weight of his responsibilities and that did something to his mind. It put the block on, somehow. Made him less proficient in the chase. If Della had been more obliging he'd have had no need to chase at all, but she'd forced it on him. And that made it doubly galling that the one or two fumbling shots he'd tried recently hadn't even come near a level of satisfaction.

Well, if all else failed there were other sources. He knew of one or two houses scattered about the town where he could get what he wanted and no questions asked. It was time he gave them a try—and damn Della.

It amused him—calmed him—to go through the list, sorting out the right brothel to try first. And working out a scheme of when and how, he fell asleep.

When Della's alarm went off half an hour later, its sound failed to penetrate the curtain of his dreams.

★ ★ ★ ★

P.C Bill Hibbert grinned at his companion across the gloomy confines of the unmarked, blue Zephyr.

'The job's bucking up, Frank,' he said. 'We've actually been *told* to park-up and watch birds at bus stops. Before now, they'd have ripped us open if they'd caught us doing this. Suddenly, it's legal. Where will it end, old mate?'

Frank Johnson's mood was less enthusiastic.

'In botching the bloody job, if you don't keep your bloody voice down,' he

58

grumbled. 'That girl keeps on looking this way and sniffing. She mightn't have seen us yet, but she'll sure as hell hear us if you keep on yapping. Any minute now, she'll start complaining about us.'

Hibbert grinned more widely.

'You're a pessimist, Frank. She hasn't heard a thing yet but there's something pulling her eyes in this direction. It's the tugging magnetism of my fatal masculinity.'

'Tugging, fatal balls.'

'That too, Frank, but I'm not boasting. For two pins I'd go over there and pull her for tonight.' He paused, musing. 'You never know, mate. There might be better things to come. They might start paying us to chat 'em up. Just imagine it—nine-to-five, woman-hunting. That's the sort of shift I could manage. They'd have me doing overtime for nowt.'

Johnson grinned his amusement.

'You'd be clapped-out inside a fortnight,' he said, 'but it'd only be mental fatigue. There's the talkers and there's the doers, Bill—and you talk too much. Anyway, you're too late. That's one bird you won't pull.'

Both men leaned forward in their seats, seeing the pretty brunette in her slim skirt step to the pavement edge with arm held out. A moment later a brightly lit double-decker blotted out her form, until she appeared again, faintly visible through smoky glass, her high heels clipping the stairs towards the top deck.

'Not bad,' Hibbert said, leering appreciatively.

'Not bad at all,' Johnson echoed, 'but bloody gone, mate. So why are we still hanging about here?'

★ ★ ★ ★

Hibbert pushed his flat cap backwards on his thatch, twisted the engine to life and moved slowly away.

A thousand yards along the main drag he turned sharp left into the first cross-thoroughfare. A half mile more and then left again, sticking to one of the town's main bus routes. Hibbert and Johnson knew all the routes and most of the stops. They cruised at a steady twenty, eyes flicking from stop to stop along the way.

Their instructions had been plain.

Check the stops and keep on checking till well into the bustle of the day. Look for isolated females waiting to board early morning buses. If you find any, park the car unobtrusively and keep watch. Maintain surveillance for as long as necessary—usually till the woman boards her bus—and then move along and look for others.

The rest of the drill had been left unsaid, but as experienced members of Crime-patrol, both officers knew exactly what action they would take if anything happened to suggest that a lone female was at risk. They had already stood guard on half-a-dozen unsuspecting women and there had been no kind of incident.

'This is a waste of bloody time,' Hibbert groused after another uneventful observation. 'There's nobody stirring at this hour.'

'Somebody's stirred seven times in the last ten days,' Johnson reminded him. 'That makes him a persistent bugger. I don't imagine he'll stop now, whoever he is.'

Hibbert nodded, serious for once.

'No, he's bound to have another go. Tell you one thing though, it's right what they were saying about these early birds. They're thick on the ground these mornings, and I always thought the girls liked getting up late. I never realised till this job started that we'd got so much spare hanging about every day, waiting for early buses. A lot more women than blokes too. It makes you wonder why.'

Johnson was keened-up, no longer listening to Hibbert's maundering. He'd seen something.

'Corner of King Street,' he whispered. 'She's standing back in the shadows, away from the stop. Nip into that alley by the Odeon. We can come back out through Whalley's Court and watch from there.'

Hibbert said nothing till he'd swept the car around a block of town-centre property and parked facing out to the main street with the car's nose in shadow. Then he hissed an objection.

'She's just a scrubber, Frank. Forty, if she's a day.'

'Life begins at forty,' Johnson said loftily. 'You bits of kids are all the same. You don't know a real woman when you see one. That one's built for it, Bill. Let her get her hooks in you, my lad, and she'll eat you for breakfast. So shut up and keep watching.'

The woman might have been a statue for all the movement she made and several minutes passed while they watched her in silence. Then Johnson hissed a warning and spoke softly.

'Coming now, Bill,' he whispered. 'On the corner of Woolworths and crossing over. That's a bloke, isn't it?'

'So it's a bloke.' Hibbert scoffed a denial of interest. 'He's done nowt to complain of yet.'

'Give him time, Bill. It takes time.'

They followed the man with their eyes, saw him step over to the bus stop and stand leaning against the lamp standard, gazing along the street. Several yards away from him, the woman continued to wait.

It was a normal, law-abiding scene, and it lasted for half a minute. After that, the man and the woman looked at each other and a smile could be seen splitting the man's face. His lips moved as though in conversation, but no sound of words reached the ears of the constables. A moment later, the man strolled casually across to the woman and slipped an arm round her waist.

Johnson sucked in an expectant breath. 'What did I tell you?' he whispered.

The woman seemed to take the man's approach good-naturedly, but she shrugged him away and moved a few paces. The man followed and again she side-stepped. Once again he reached out to her, and this time, almost by accident it appeared, he took hold of the strap of her shoulder bag. Once more she seemed to protest, tugging at the captured strap and striking a leisurely, fending blow.

'What about it, Frank?' Hibbert whispered.

'That's quite enough for me, Bill,' Johnson said. 'I'm going to have words with that bugger.'

Johnson eased his heavy frame out of the police car, closed the door gently and tip-toed towards the developing scene. For ten yards he went unnoticed. Then his feet struck against something on the pavement and there was an unholy clinking and rattling.

Blasted milk bottles!

The two at the bus stop had seen him now.

The woman made startled sound without words, but she stayed. Not so the man. He took to his heels suddenly and fast, haring away towards the Market Square, his feet thudding on the tarmac. Johnson didn't even try to pursue.

'Grab him, Bill,' he shouted, and was

rewarded to see the police car swerve jerkily into the main street and roar off on the track of the runner, gaining perceptibly.

Johnson carried on walking—approached the woman.

'What was all that about, love?' he said.

CHAPTER 6

Johnson and Hibbert were disappointed men and the woman was not particularly pleased either.

Sitting in the interview room at Cotteston Police Station, she reacted angrily to a string of patient questions from Trevor Berry, the morning sergeant. Her main concern was being late for work.

'What ever am I going to tell Mr Fellowes when his office hasn't been cleaned?' she moaned. 'I'll get my cards for this, and it'll be all through you lot.'

'We'll sort it out for you, Mrs Sephton,' Berry promised. 'I'll ring your firm myself and explain. Only we've had a lot of trouble lately, with women being molested.

We've got to try to catch whoevers' doing it. You can't blame my men, you know. This chap was giving you a bad time, wasn't he?'

The woman seemed affronted.

'Give over, Sergeant,' she scoffed. 'You think it's the first time I've ever had a pass made? Time enough to worry when they *stop* doing it. I'm quite capable of looking after myself you know, without the bobbies butting in.'

'You like that sort of thing, do you?' Berry said, allowing his bitterness to rule his tongue.

'I didn't say that. But I'm no man-hater, Sergeant. They'll get no change out of me, don't you worry, but I'm not one to complain because they try.'

The interview had been going on for the best part of an hour. Berry was getting nowhere fast, and he knew it.

'You've no wish to complain then?' he said in desperation.

'Course not. Why should I? There's no harm done.'

'But doesn't it upset you when a complete stranger grabs hold of you in the street and starts messing about? Doesn't it frighten you?'

'How should I know, Sergeant? It hasn't happened yet.'

'Oh, come on now, Mrs Sephton...'

'I'm not a liar, Sergeant. It hasn't happened.'

'But two of my own men saw it happen.'

'Your two nosy bobbies saw a friendly chat, that's all, and what's to be frightened about in that? If you must know, he wasn't a stranger.'

Not a stranger?

Berry was quick to clutch the point as a life-saving straw. It was the worst of luck that the man had eluded young Hibbert—that men on foot could dodge along bollarded footways where police cars couldn't follow. It had been a near miss, but all they had to show for it was a thin and tatty description of the man. A description that might have fitted just about anybody. But if the woman knew...

'Are you saying you know who he is?' he asked hopefully.

She seemed to regret having spoken.

'More or less—yes. Well, not who he is, exactly, but I know him well enough.'

'That's fine then. Tell me about him.'

'Why should I?' The woman sounded very determined. 'He's done nothing. I tell you. Can't have you hounding a poor chap who's done nothing.'

Berry stifled his next question before it left his lips.

He felt on safer ground now. The woman knew something. She wasn't going to pass it over on a plate, but she'd give eventually. But he'd antagonised her already, and chances were she'd keep her mouth shut just to spite him. What he needed now was one of the girls to tease information out of the woman by a more feminine approach.

He checked his watch. Ten minutes to nine. Jenny Collinge was on duty at nine and that meant she'd probably have arrived already. He opened the door of the interview room and bellowed:-

'Jenny!'

There was an immediate, reassuring reply.

'Coming, Sarge.'

★ ★ ★ ★

It sometimes happens—though not always by any means—that a female complainant will talk more freely to a woman than to a man. Mrs Sephton was not easily

68

cajoled, but Jenny persisted. And during the next half hour a few more useful facts emerged.

It wasn't a lot—but it was something. As soon as she felt she had something new—Jenny reported back to Sergeant Berry.

'No name or address, Sarge, but she knows him all right. Apparently she's seen him many a time, over the years. He's bought her a few drinks in local pubs, danced with her, things like that. She swears all this happened before she was married, but she's been married eleven years now, so I'd take that with a pinch of salt.'

'Sounds as if he's been knocking her off,' Berry said.

'No. I don't think it's anything like that. They've just met casually, in mixed company. If it was any deeper than that, she'd surely know who he is and where he comes from.'

'Yes, and if I know her type, she'd keep it to herself.' Berry scowled. 'You're quite sure she doesn't know?'

'Sure as I can be. I think she's telling the truth.'

'I'll take your word for it, Jenny, though

I'm still doubtful. And he wasn't going for her handbag either?'

'She says not. She says it was an accident, and I believe her. In fact, she hadn't even thought about it till I mentioned it to her. Then she remembered he was making a playful grab at her when the strap got in the way. He didn't tug it or anything, and when she swung at him, he let go.'

Berry considered the facts.

'All right then,' he said, 'but what bugs me a bit is why the silly bugger ran away. If it was all plain sailing as the woman says, why didn't he just stay there and explain? Why did he take off like that?'

Jenny grinned.

'Come on, Sarge. You know better than that. It means he must be a married man, wouldn't you think? He wouldn't dare admit messing about with a woman in case his wife found out. I'll bet that was his main reason.'

'Not just scared of the police, then?'

'I'm not sure. He might have been. Just before Frank Johnson showed up she'd told the chap to clear off or she'd shout for the bobbies. It was only said as a joke, she tells me, but when Frank appeared he must have thought it was ominous.'

'The fact remains that he ran', Berry insisted, 'and blokes who run away are asking to be chased. I don't give a damn what their reason is. I can't forget that woman last week, Jenny. She ran, poor sod, and it might have been this bugger that made her run. So we want him. He can come here and answer a few questions. You got a description?'

'Yes. A bit of one. It makes him seem very ordinary though. No special features or anything like that. Wait a minute, though.' She skimmed quickly through her notes. 'Yes, here it is. Do you know a man called Harry Jenks?'

'No. Why?'

'She says he's a mate of his. I had to practically drag it out of her. You mustn't forget, Sergeant, she's married too. Half the reason why she won't help is because she's frightened what her husband might think.'

'Where does Jenks live?'

'She says she doesn't know. If you want my opinion, she's lying about that, but I tried to shake her and I couldn't.'

'Never mind, Jenny. You've done a good job. We can always ask around and see if anybody knows Jenks. Is there anything else you can tell me?'

'About the bloke at the bus stop? Well, his dress might be a bit of a lead. He was wearing a tweed jacket, blue trousers that she thought were part of a uniform, and black boots.'

'Boots?'

'That's right, Sarge. Heavy ones. The kind some of our lads wear.'

★ ★ ★ ★

At eleven o'clock that day, yet another report of a handbag theft came in.

The victim reported it in person and Berry himself took the initial complaint at the public counter. He looked the woman over as he probed for details. She was in her early thirties, a garment-presser at a local factory. Berry checked his watch and decided that this job was a foreigner, not part of the current sequence, because the timing was all wrong.

Well, it didn't surprise him. There were plenty of thieves about and it didn't have to be the same man.

He was taking a description of the missing bag when the woman startled him with her forthrightness.

'You can also write that he shoved his hand up my skirt.'

Berry eyed her warily.

'Did you get a good look at him?' he asked.

'No. It was nearly pitch dark.'

Berry glanced pointedly at the window through which the sun's rays beamed.

'Dark?'

'That's right, dark. I didn't say it had just happened, Sergeant. It happened at half past six this morning.'

★ ★ ★ ★

After the woman had gone, Berry summoned Frank Johnson and Bill Hibbert and gave instructions.

'Go to Empress Road,' he said, 'the bus stop just up from the chip-shop. Look round for a handbag. Try the back street, the yard walls, the gardens. You know the drill by now.'

'When did it happen?' Hibbert asked.

Berry told him.

'Bloody hell, Sarge. Empress Road's

more than a mile from our job at the Odeon. Looks as though it can't have been the same bloke.'

'What time did your job happen, Bill?'

'Just after seven.'

'And how long does it take to cover a mile?'

'Damned if I know, Sarge.'

'Well I do,' Berry snapped. 'Fifteen minutes at a steady walk—and if you're a fast runner, four bloody minutes. So there you are, Bill, you daft bugger. He could have made it walking on his hands. It's the same bloke all right. When you and Frank disturbed him he was on his second go of the morning.'

★ ★ ★ ★

The Crime-car was back at base within half an hour.

Hibbert looked just a touch sheepish as he held out a black leather handbag by its strap, offering it to Berry.

Berry grinned.

'What did I tell you, Bill? I knew he'd have thrown the bugger away. One thing's absolutely certain lads, this bugger isn't after handbags.'

CHAPTER 7

It was broad daylight when Colin Duffy reached home by a roundabout route. He'd hurried most of the way, making up time, but he covered the last hundred yards at a steady walk, cautiously checking the street for signs of unusual movement. There were a few people about, but they were minding their own business. Not policemen, he felt sure.

He'd been late home a few times recently, but never quite so late as this, and he might need an excuse. He could always say he'd worked late for some reason—and there wasn't much risk that Della would check up on him. But what reason? Well, if he had to cross that bridge he'd think of a reason, and with a bit of luck it wouldn't be necessary.

Della was wide awake when he bore his morning coffee into the bedroom. The light was on already. She glanced at her wrist watch and gave him an accusing look.

'Where the devil have you been, Col? You're nearly an hour late.'

'Knocking off another woman, dearest,' he said brusquely, 'where the hell do you think?'

She snuggled back under the sheets, a disbelieving smirk on her face, and Duffy breathed more easily. If she'd pressed him it might not have been easy to palm her off...but she hadn't pressed him.

He undressed quickly, switched the light out and slid into the bed alongside her. For a while he lay stick-rigid, completely forgetting to make his usual overtures, and then his troubled wits told him that if he didn't do something she'd think it odd. He reached an arm across her warm body, stroking, murmuring, waiting for the inevitable refusal and harsh words that would follow.

But Della surprised him for once.

This time there was no drawing away, no grumbles about timing and no vague promises to the future. This time she faced him, received him.

And it was great.

★ ★ ★ ★

76

When it was over she left him in bed while she dressed and went downstairs to busy herself with breakfast for the kids. He watched her dressing, loved the matter-of-fact way she stripped her nightdress away and strolled naked about the room, picking up wisps of nylon and dragging them over her pink body. Della was still a fetching piece. The years and the pregnancies hadn't changed that. Get her in the right frame of mind and he'd rather have Della than any of the other women he knew.

Duffy was tired out now, satiated, but wakefulness lingered as his thoughts ranged over the events of the morning, beginning with the last half-hour.

Coming home late had brought an unexpected reward in the shape of a much more amenable wife. Perhaps there was a lesson to be learned there. A wide awake Della was an approachable Della—as satisfactory a mate as he could ever have wished for. So the experiment might be worth repeating. He'd have to organise things so that he came late to bed more often, if only by waiting downstairs for a while to give her time to surface properly.

He didn't want too many scares like this morning, though. He was getting a bit too old for that sort of thing and he might not be so lucky next time.

He smiled in the darkness, remembering his brief and breathless flight. Christ! It must be getting on twenty years since he'd run away from a bobby, and in the intervening time he'd more than once been the chaser rather than the chased. But the feeling had been much the same. His ageing limbs had responded magnificently as they'd done years ago when he'd more than once rushed for safety, clutching an unlicensed air-gun or a shirtful of stolen apples.

Neither the wings of fear nor the guile of evasion had deserted him, and by ducking away through the maze of remembered alleyways he'd shaken off the hunt as effectively as always.

Whether or not he'd been right to run was an unanswerable question, but if he hadn't run there'd surely have been an awkward ten minutes of explanation. She might have backed him or she might not. It depended on how vengeful or otherwise the woman might have been.

She hadn't exactly repulsed him.

She'd brushed him off, all right, but in a way she'd been egging him on too, and the half smile on her lips had had something of the come hither about it. He didn't know whether she was easy meat or not, but he'd heard rumours that suggested she might be—and she wasn't the kind you'd turn your nose up at.

He remembered her well enough.

He'd met her an odd time or two in the past, swanning round the local pubs, and a few drinks and the feel of her lively body gyrating through a waltz or a quick-step had made her seem forthcoming. Seeing her at the bus stop had brought those memories back into sharp focus, caused him to linger there, poised as a passenger in the hope that old acquaintances might still be worth something. Maybe if he'd caught her some other place—not at a bus stop—she might have...

The woman was still on his mind when he fell asleep, and his last thought was a resolve.

He'd have to look her up again in different circumstances. She was on his list now, as a definite possibility.

★ ★ ★ ★

'You must have been fairly close to him at one stage, Frank. Could you recognise him again?'

It was ten o'clock that same morning and the latest bus stop incident was being discussed in Detective Inspector Wilson's office. Frank Johnson and Bill Hibbert, feeling a little out of place among a gaggle of jacks, were being cross-examined. Detective Sergeant Matt Hollis and Detective Constable Jack Reade were more relaxed in what was to them a familiar atmosphere and Jenny Collinge, with the aplomb common to her sex, felt no strain at all in the company of men.

Wilson asked the question. Johnson scratched his head and did his best to answer it.

'Not on a line-up, sir, that's for sure,' he admitted. 'Those sodium lights aren't the best things for giving you a good look at people. I've told you what he looked like, but too many men look like that. I'd go along with the boots and uniform trousers—his jacket was a lot lighter coloured than his pants anyway—but beyond that I don't think I could help a lot.'

Wilson accepted the set-back with hardly a flicker. He turned to Hibbert.

'How about you, Bill?'

'I can't remember much, sir. His build—and roughly his dress—yes. But I've no real picture of his face. I was too busy watching what he was doing.'

'There's the woman, sir,' Jenny pointed out. 'She says she knows him well enough.'

'Will she pick him out, though?' Wilson doubted.

'She'd need a lot of persuading. She could if she wanted to, but she doesn't want to, and the reason's fairly obvious.'

'You mean because she's married?'

'No. If it were only that, we could talk her into helping by promising to keep it quiet. But as far as she's concerned the man did nothing she objected to, so why should she help us to find him? As she sees it, we ought to leave him alone and forget about it.'

'You explained to her about the others?' Wilson queried.

'Yes, I told her, but she won't believe it of him. If there's a man going round attacking women it isn't this man. She says he wouldn't have bothered her at all if she hadn't spoken to him and smiled at him. They knew each other, you see.'

Wilson nodded knowingly.

'She was encouraging him, was she? Giving him the glad eye?'

Jenny frowned in thought.

'I think there was a bit of that, but she denies it. According to her, she spoke to him because she recognised him. She's quite adamant that there was no need for anybody to interfere. She feels quite sure he'd have left her alone as soon as the bus came.'

'And what about this other name she gave you?'

'Harry Jenks? Well, I don't know. We've asked around but nobody seems to have heard of him. I'm beginning to think she made the name up just to confuse us, though to be fair I thought it was the truth when she said it.'

'What about the burgess list?'

'No joy so far, sir,' Matt Hollis put in. 'Mind you it's a hell of a job and Jenks isn't all that uncommon a name. We're doing the town hall records as well, but we're not making much progress.'

'Well, keep at it. Now we know he had

hold of her handbag at one stage. Any hopes of prints?'

'No sir,' Hollis said. 'He only grabbed the strap, and it turns out to be a fibre weave. The lads have dusted it, but they can't even find fingermarks, let alone detail.'

'And you've let her go Matt, I understand?'

'That's right sir. We'd no reason to hold her, since she wouldn't push a complaint. I had a good go at her first, about the chance that he might be the man responsible for other jobs and I told her that by covering for him she might be putting other women at risk, but like Jenny says, she wouldn't wear it at any price.'

'We don't *have* to have a complaint,' Wilson pointed out. 'Not if there's other independent evidence. And let's face it, both Johnson and Hibbert saw it happen.'

'That's fair enough sir,' Hollis agreed, 'but you've got to admit it was all a bit mild. Suppose we found the bloke and charged him. We'd have precious little chance of a conviction, even for common assault, with the woman batting against us.'

It was an obvious truth. Wilson accepted

it and dropped the argument.

'All right, Matt, but we've got a string of other jobs on our plate. He fits the description we've had from other women, doesn't he?'

'Yes and no,' Hollis told him. 'He isn't outside the frame by any means, but we haven't got half enough details to say more. He might have damn all to do with any of them.'

'Just the same, I want the bugger found,' Wilson insisted. 'These morning assaults are getting too regular for my liking and up to now this is the best lead we've had. We won't get anywhere if we don't push our leads. This uniform bit, for instance,' he paused and cast a lowering look at his subordinates. 'He wasn't one of our lads, I trust?'

Hibbert answered him with some conviction.

'No sir, definitely not. Not from this Division anyway, or I'd have known him straight off. I suppose he could be from outside, but what would a bobby be doing off his patch at that hour of the morning—and wearing Huggins' flannels?'

'Maybe he lives on us?' Reade suggested.

'He doesn't, Jack,' Hibbert said firmly. 'Not unless he's only moved in recently. We've only got four outside bobbies living on the patch, two from Merseyside and two from Greater Manchester, and I know all four well enough.'

'So it must have been some other sort of uniform,' Wilson said. 'A fireman or something.'

'Trouble is, there are so many possibilities,' Matt Hollis said. 'I've listed one or two. Bus crew, train crew, ambulanceman, meterman, postman, private security firm, works policeman, as well as the fireman or policeman, you've already mentioned. And it doesn't stop there, either. They've got a nice line in surplus police trousers at the Army and Navy Stores, on sale to anybody. So it's no use pretending it's going to be easy.'

'All right, all right,' Wilson said, irritated, 'but we've got to start somewhere, or this bugger's going to beat us. I'm looking for bright ideas.'

'How about doing a watch, sir?' Johnson suggested.

'A watch, Frank? What the hell on?'

'On the same bus stop, sir. When me and Bill first saw him he came to the stop and stood there waiting. He must have been there a minute or so before he started freshing up the woman, so chances are he uses the stop every morning. I reckon it's worth a try.'

Wilson's face relaxed a little. The idea sounded useful to him. But Jenny Collinge had other ideas.

'It won't work,' she said.

'Why not, Jenny?'

'Because it's the other way round, sir. It's the woman, not the man, who uses that stop every day. If he used it as well, they'd see each other regularly and there'd be no need for all that messing about. Either they'd be on a lot better terms or else he'd have burned his fingers long ago. I ask you, Frank. I've listened to you describing what happened. It doesn't sound to me as though they see each other every morning. What do you think?'

'Not when you put it that way,' Johnson admitted. 'Unless he waited till this particular morning to chance his arm, and that's stretching things a bit too far.'

'Which brings us back to the woman,' Wilson said grimly. 'Sooner or later we're going to have to see that bitch again.'

CHAPTER 8

Scrambling down the steep grass bank beside the dirty waters of Cotteston Beck, he fumbled in the cracked culvert wall and took out the handbag.

It was a shiny affair in black plastic, with a silver-metal clasp and moccasin stitching round the edges. There was a raw break in the thin strap, caused when she'd gripped tight and he'd had to wrench it from her.

He couldn't think why he'd kept the thing instead of chucking it away unopened like he'd done with all the others. Opening it had been a sop to his curiosity, but something he'd found inside had made him hang on to it. He hadn't quite sorted out the reason yet.

It wasn't the bundle of notes, though thirty quid was thirty quid and being flush with money was never a hardship. No, it had to be the photograph. It did things for him. He opened the bag, fumbled for the photograph and looked at it.

It showed a very shapely young woman, bikini-clad, sunning herself on a lawn, with one leg bent at the knee and breasts bulging over her folded arms in a meaty vee. That was certainly it.

That—and the letter.

He opened the letter again and read it through, grinning at the purple passages. It was bloody hot stuff. Not the sort he'd ever have written to a girl, if ever he'd thought of writing to girls. But he wished he could have written such a letter, and he wished the things it described had happened to him with a girl, especially the girl in the photo.

Next he took out the diary, thumbed through it and read the scant entries done in small, neat writing. Nothing much in the diary though—not a patch on the letter. But there was a name and address inside the front cover—and there was a telephone number. He could have some fun with that.

He slipped the diary into his pocket, stuffed the rest back inside the handbag and slipped the bag into its hiding place. Then he set off in search of a telephone kiosk.

★ ★ ★ ★

Rosemary Sanderson was in her bath when the phone rang.

She ignored it at first. Mother would answer it and shout upstairs if it was for her. But when the strident sound persisted and the expected rattle of the handset didn't come, Rosemary remembered. She was alone in the house. Mother had gone out shopping.

Bother the phone.

She wasn't expecting a call. If she had been—and if it had been from somebody important—she'd have gone downstairs in a flash. But whoever it was would just have to call again when she was better prepared to respond. She splashed her legs with blue water, growing more and more curious as the ringing continued. After a minute, her curiosity got the better of her. She rose dripping from the bath, wrapped a towel about her and padded down the stairs.

She lifted the phone to her ear.

'Hello. Who is it?'

A man's voice answered—an unfamiliar voice.

'Mrs Sanderson?'

She might have known it wasn't for her, drat the thing.

'No. My mother's out, I'm afraid. Can I help?'

'It's Rosemary Sanderson I want.'

'Oh. Well, I'm Rosemary.'

There was a short period of silence, then the man said:-

'It's about your handbag. You lost it the other day.'

'I didn't lose it—I had it stolen.'

'Same difference, isn't it?'

He sounded a bit lippy. She answered in kind.

'You might think so, but I don't. Anyway, what business is it of yours?'

'Plenty, Rosemary. I've got it.'

What right had he to use first names, the cheeky thing? Still, there wasn't much point in getting huffy.

'What do you mean, you've got it?'

'Don't mess about, girl. I've got the bloody thing haven't I? I found it.'

'Where did you find it?'

'Never mind that. Do you want it back?'

'Yes I do. The police do anyway. If you really have got it, why don't you take it to the police station and hand it in?'

90

'Not a chance, Rosemary. I'll give it to you, or nobody.'

'All right then,' she said, exasperated, 'give it to me.'

'What's it worth if I do?'

She hesitated before replying. He sounded greedy and not at all helpful. And yet she supposed it was a fair enough question. If he'd found it he'd be looking for some sort of reward, and after all it was a good class handbag. She'd gladly pay a couple of pounds to get it back, and if the money was still in it she could afford to be more generous. But was the money still there?

'That depends,' she said guardedly. 'In the first place, how do I know you've really got it?'

'I've got your name, haven't I? And your telephone number? How would I know that if I hadn't got it? Anyway, how would I know you'd even lost a handbag?'

'All right. If you've got it, tell me what's in it.'

'Well, let's see. There's a photo of you. You're a nice looking kid, Rosemary. A big girl, too. Yummy.'

'What else?' she said, ignoring his personal remarks.

'A diary, lipstick, comb, handkerchief.'

'Any money?'

'Yes. Thirty quid.'

All of it still there. That was good news.

'Bring it to me and you can have a fiver,' she offered.

'Come off it, girl. What's a bloody fiver? I can keep the whole thirty if I want.'

Of course he could. But if he'd wanted to do that he needn't have rung up in the first place. So why had he bothered. He didn't sound like an honest man. Rosemary started to feel uncomfortable.

'All right,' she said with a show of reluctance, 'make it a tenner. Or better still, bring it here and I'll split the money fifty-fifty.'

'That's more like it, Rosemary,' he said, 'but it's still not good enough.'

'How much do you want, then?'

'I don't want money. I want something else.'

He said it pointedly, as though tracing lines to spell out a message in between. Rosemary was pretty sure she could read the message. Her immediate reaction was to slam the phone down and refuse to answer any further calls. Even with the money in it, the handbag wasn't

92

worth another minute of this dubious conversation. And yet she felt compelled to stay with the phone—to ask the obvious question.

'Go on, then. What is it you're after?'

The man chuckled in a nasty way.

'Well, it's like this. I've been reading this letter of yours. It's very good, Rosemary, but you don't look that sort of girl. Who's this bloke Stephen?'

Oh God! Stephen's letter.

Stephen had been an idiot to write such a letter in the first place, and if anything, she'd been a bigger fool for not tearing it into strips and flushing it down the loo. But she'd opened it when her mother was looking and she'd hidden it along with her blushes by stuffing it into her handbag. She'd forgotten about it till now—and now this man had it, he'd read it. Heaven alone knew what he must think about it—and about her. Rosemary squirmed in the muddy waters of her own thoughts. A hot denial of that damning letter sprang to her lips but she knew it would be useless to voice it. Useless to explain that much of Stephen's fanciful prose was wild exaggeration—which it certainly was—but equally useless to deny it was based on pretty glaring indiscretions on her part, since that also was true. Now, more than ever, she wanted to slam the phone down and return to the bathroom in a fit of sulks.

But she felt an overriding urge to get the better of this situation if she could.

She kept the conversation going on an even plane, pleaded, cajoled and allowed herself to be drawn reluctantly into a bargaining position. The man was only too happy to bargain. Once they'd reached agreement, the call ended.

And Rosemary dried herself, dressed and went to Cotteston Police Station.

★ ★ ★ ★

The policeman she really wanted was Sergeant Toban.

Apart from anything else, she wanted to apologise to Toban for having called him kinky, because now she felt quite sure that Toban had been right about the handbag thief.

But Toban was off duty. Rosemary shopped around having cryptic conversations with various policemen, until she found herself facing Detective Sergeant Hollis across his desk. She decided to talk to Hollis. She told him everything—or nearly everything. She couldn't bring herself to mention the letter.

'Did he give a name or anything?' Hollis asked.

'No. I asked him but he wouldn't say.'

'What about his voice? Did you pick up any impressions from the way he spoke?'

'No, not really. I'd say he was a young man, but I could be wrong there. I'm convinced it was the same man, though.'

'The man who attacked you? Why do you say that?'

'I don't know. It's just a feeling I've got. I accused him of it over the phone and he just laughed. I think that's what convinced me, the way he laughed. He didn't deny anything—and he would have, if it wasn't him.'

'All right then. Now tell me what you arranged.'

'I said I'd meet him in Queen's Park at four o'clock this afternoon. He said he'd bring the bag with him and hand it over.'

'Just like that? Didn't he want anything for it?'

She hesitated.

'Look, Sergeant. You've got to understand I was just playing him along. I wouldn't ever have done it.'

'Done what?' he said, puzzled. 'You're not explaining things very well.'

'I promised I'd have sex with him.'

Matt Hollis was surprised but he tried not to show it. She was a nurse, of course, and perhaps a bit more forthright than most because of her profession.

'Did you make it sound convincing?' he asked.

'Yes. I think so. I told him he could have the money if he'd give me the handbag back, but not the other thing. I cried a bit and pleaded a bit, and then I sort of gave way slowly. I said I couldn't do what he wanted at any price, then I said I'd think about it, then after a long time I said if he'd give me everything back, the money as well, I'd do it and not tell anybody. I'm sure he believed me.'

He was more surprised than ever. That sort of conversation must have been a hell of an ordeal, but she'd handled it better than a trained policewoman. Hollis couldn't help admiring her.

'You said he rang from a call-box?' he said.

'That's right. I heard the pips at the beginning.'

'But he must have been on the line a long time?'

'Yes, he was. He had to keep feeding tuppenny bits into the slot. You can always hear them dropping.'

There was only one important question remaining. Matt Hollis studied the girl in silence for an instant. Then he asked the question.

'Are you ready to see this thing right through?'

'Yes. That's why I came here.' She grinned faintly. 'But I've no intention of keeping that promise I made.'

★ ★ ★ ★

Detective Inspector Wilson had high hopes of success from this latest development. He and Hollis organised their men and set the scene with care.

But the squib fizzled briefly and went out.

An hour before the due time, sitting impatiently at home, Rosemary Sanderson received another call from the same man.

'You've put the cops on me,' he said.

'I haven't. Why should I?'

He was swearing a lot more this time, coarse words that she knew but wouldn't have dreamed of using.

'Don't give me that,' he said between expletives. 'I watched you go in there in those green slacks of yours. You're better looking than your picture, Rosemary, even if you are such a bloody sneaky little bitch.'

He went on to describe her in unpleasant detail. Miserably, she stood with the phone to her ear, waiting till the tirade ended.

'What about my handbag?' she asked, lamely.

'You've had that,' he told her bluntly. 'You got it the wrong way round, Rosemary. You should have opened your legs and kept your bloody mouth shut.'

★ ★ ★ ★

She'd been very wrong to keep anything back from Sergeant Hollis. When she spoke to him again to explain the uselessness of going ahead with the plan, she also told him about the letter.

★ ★ ★ ★

And Matt Hollis reported to a very disgruntled Wilson.

'The bastard,' Wilson cursed. 'He must have been somewhere right outside the nick to see her come in. This bugger's playing with us, Matt.'

'What happens next, though? What about the letter?'

'It's pretty strong meat, is it?'

'I gather so, sir. She wouldn't go into detail. In fact I told her not to. But in general terms it's not the sort of thing she'd want her mother to get hold of—or her employers for that matter.'

'Would it be good enough for blackmail?'

'If he made the right sort of threats, she'd be very unhappy about it. Mind you, I've drummed it into her that she mustn't do anything without telling us. I've given her my home telephone number. She can ring me or the missus any time, and I can't see this clever bugger finding that out. Do you reckon he'd try blackmail?'

'You know as much as I do, Matt,' Wilson said. 'He seems versatile enough to me. I reckon he'd turn his hand to anything in the book.'

CHAPTER 9

There was agonizing pain as the girl sank her sharp teeth into the pad of his palm.

She was a nicely made piece, young and with puppy fat still clinging, but it clung in all the right places. Even at first view, from thirty yards away, he'd had her taped as one of the best-looking he'd picked on so far. The short red coat, belted at the waist, had shown off her figure rather than covered it, and the nonchalant way she'd leaned against the lamp, hip jutting aggressively, had filled him with a familiar lust.

He'd come up to her neatly from behind while she was staring sleepily into the distance and he hadn't even bothered to pretend that he was interested in her handbag. He felt the warmth of her at once, and the smoothness. Her breasts felt firm, real, and her young buttocks wriggled sexily against him as he closed with her and the struggle began.

But she protested on a mighty penetrating note.

One hand was cupped tightly over a single breast and he felt it expand puffily as she gathered air, so he knew the sound was coming. But before he could transfer his other hand from waist to mouth she let forth with that one scream, a shrill, piercing din.

And then she bit his hand.

But he knew she'd go on screaming unless he stopped her, so the hand across her mouth was vitally necessary, and even though her razor teeth kept slashing at his palm he held the hand firmly in place.

Had anyone heard the scream, he wondered?

The road itself in both directions was a palely lighted ribbon—empty. A hundred yards away, on a raised site overlooking the road, there was a long row of terraced houses. But they were in darkness and stayed that way. Behind him there was a long narrow strip of grassland, thinly wooded, and beyond the haggard saplings a railway-sleeper fence. No houses beyond the fence and no receptive ears. Only darkness and stillness.

But somebody, somewhere, might have

heard the commotion, so he'd better move the girl away, just in case. The spot where they struggled was right on the edge of the coned light from the nearest street lamp and if anyone looked in that direction they'd certainly be seen. Firming his grip around her chest and keeping the gag in place against her mobile teeth, he began to drag her back from the roadway, weaving a path between the trees.

She fought him every inch of the way, arching and twisting her body against his hold, hacking at his ankles with her bulky wedge shoes and always biting, gnawing, slashing at the searing hot chunk of pain that was his palm. The bloody woman had rabbit teeth—and sharp ones at that. The sheer effort of dulling his mind against the stab of wounded flesh was more agonizing than the pain itself.

Yet he dared not free her. If he removed the sore hand as his brain kept urging him to do, she'd scream and scream, and the capacity of her lungs was impressive. He began to rue the moment when he'd chosen to tackle this one. A few of his earlier victims had screamed, but none so noisily as this bellows-chested bitch.

He held on with the strength of

desperation, squeezing, squeezing, willing her to be silent. He clenched his own teeth until they ached, steeling himself against the pain in his hand, and all the time he looked round for a likely avenue of flight. The feel of her body writhing against his was no longer the exciting sensation it had been. He'd had as much of her as he'd ever wanted, and if only she'd stop biting and struggling he'd be happy to turn her loose and run for safety.

But it was too late for that.

Suddenly there was a more urgent need to stifle her cries. The sound of an approaching bus grew louder in his ears and the bright lights of its windows burst on the scene as though activated by a switch. He could see the radiant pool of light glinting through the trees, rushing towards him like a roving searchlight. Any second now, he'd be nakedly visible, and it was no longer possible to run.

There was a broad gap in the sleeper fence. He'd noticed it earlier and mentally marked it off as a useful route, but in the stress of the occasion its proximity had slipped his mind. But he could see the gap now, right at his elbow, and its presence gave him new hope. He summoned reserves of energy to heave her, kicking and struggling, through the gap and fling her down a steep weed-covered bank, still clutching her body to his. Locked in a wriggling embrace they rolled over and over till they came to rest at the bottom of a dry ditch, his body pinning hers against a tangle of vegetation.

But the girl had seen the approaching bus too, and she redoubled her efforts to escape from his grasp, grinding her teeth into the flesh of his hand and wriggling her hot body along the length of him. He straddled her now, face to face in the classic sexual pose with one arm still looped about her neck and the suffering palm still pressed against her chewing teeth. Would this silly bitch never stop biting? He pressed harder and tried to forget the pain.

And it worked—something worked. The hunger was coming back to him and in the face of the hunger the pain receded. He felt his body responding fiercely to the unintentional arousal impulses generated by the struggling woman. Her thighs scissored beneath his thighs, her firm chest heaved its twin hills against his own chest and her thick, dark hair brushed and chafed against his face.

And the smell of her. The sweetness of applied perfume mingled excitingly with the reek of body sweat. The clean, dark tresses filled his nostrils with their distinctive odour. The moist smoothness of her cheeks tingled against his fingers and although he could feel the persistent flexing of her jaws he was less aware of the soreness in the centre of his palm.

For the first time, he spoke to her, pressing his face against the cushion of her hair and hissing the words.

'Be still, damn you,' he said. 'I won't do you any harm if you'll just be quiet and lie still.'

Impossible for the woman to speak, yet he had his reply. Her teeth still tore at his flesh and there was no lessening in the intensity of her struggles.

There came a moment of greatest danger, when the lights from the now stationary bus shone like a beacon between the wooden blocks of the fence and when the clear voices of passengers rang in the morning air. Chattering, laughing voices. The voices of people without care, who knew nothing of the drama taking place a few short yards away.

And afterwards when the bell tinkled twice and the bus moved slowly away and began to gather speed—silence once more, and darkness.

The man grinned invisibly and closed his mind against pain. The silent world was his to enjoy, now that danger had passed. He'd seen the nasty minutes through and now he was master of the situation—master of the firm, warm body that struggled in his grasp. But with the passing of the bus, the woman seemed to have lost the will to resist. Abruptly, the biting stopped, her struggles ceased and she became limp in his hands.

Too limp. Too drained of resistance.

She'd fainted on him, the graceless cow.

And that changed things a great deal. The peak of desire had been reached and passed so that now, with his victim hushed and immobile, desire receded and became nothing. Yet he felt no sense of frustration or of dissatisfaction—rather was this the calmness that comes afterwards. A wild session—as erotic as he could ever have wished—was over and done with. But it had happened—and there would be sweet memories.

Tenderly he eased his hand from her lax mouth and pushed himself upright. For a few seconds he waited, watched the faint outline of her body in case it should move. Her stillness might be a falsity, a ruse. But she lay rigid and still, her voice no longer a source of danger.

So he left her lying there.

Scrambling up the steep bank away from the ditch, his hands encountered a square of soft, bulky leather. Her handbag. Well, it was his if he wanted it, but of course he had never wanted handbags or anything they might contain. Even if there was money in there, as there surely would be, he had no desire for that kind of riches. He still had the thirty quid from that other scheming bitch and he hadn't really wanted it. He'd just kept it out of pique.

Lifting the bag by it's strap, he swung it bolas-fashion and released it. It flew high across the ditch and away into the darkness. She'd never find it there, but serve her right and damn her to hell. When the silly cow woke, she'd have to walk to wherever she was going.

He climbed through the fence without a backward glance, to stand among the slender trees and warily examine the road. It was still quite deserted. The time was fast coming when people would be on the move, motor vehicles passing the spot in a steady stream, but the time was not yet.

Before heading for home, he paused under a street lamp, unclenched his hand and anxiously studied the ravaged palm. There were tooth punctures all over it, from the thumb-butt to the first joints of his fingers, and blood welled out of a score of jagged wounds. The pain seemed to be more pronounced now, pulsating with the berating of his heart, and the sight of his own mangled flesh shocked him.

'Jesus wept!' he said aloud. 'Jesus bloody wept.'

★ ★ ★ ★

Arthur Bracegirdle had time on his hands as the train bore him onward through miles of moving landscape.

A tiny figure in the fat nose of the nine-fifty out of Manchester, he was responsible for the safety of the train and of everything, everybody it contained. But still he had time. The rattle and motion suited him well enough and he wore the pressures of his office easily—light as a filmy mantle of gauze.

He'd always wanted to be a train driver, ever since he'd been old enough to recognise a train. As a boy, he'd lavished all his pocket money on bus fares and platform tickets to visit most of the main line stations and glory in the sight of ponderous, atlas-strong locomotives, towing goods and passengers to all parts of the country. Every train had somebody in the cab and he'd made his mind up to be that person some day. Never once, through the whole of his life, had he wavered from that ambition.

And now he was standing where he'd always wanted to be. He wasn't just a train driver, he was one of the best and most experienced in the business. These diesels were not the clanking beasts of the past, of course. Engineering wonders they might be, in their own way, but they were a whole lot simpler, more easy to operate, than the complicated and temperamental monsters of the steam age. They had to be stopped and started at the right times and places and a few minor adjustments were sometimes called for in between, but that apart, there was no real work to do.

He needed to keep checking that things were going right and that there were no problems of timing track control or mechanical breakdown.

But when there were no such problems —which was most of the time—he could spend long minutes gazing out of the window, soaking up the passing scene. It was an innocent pastime that never palled. In spite of having ridden these particular rails thousands of times and being so familiar with the route, he could always find something new to enjoy.

Arthur Bracegirdle delighted in noticing the smallest changes as they happened: a building demolished or a new one taking shape; a draining and ditching operation in the fields; a change of crops; a sowing or a harvesting, and in particular the changing of the seasons in steady, inevitable progress.

His eyes saw nature in her developing moods. The dry periods when streams filled with flowers and fresh fields became parched and brown. The coming of rain, when streams turned muddy and ran bank-high, sometimes spilling over to inundate the land. As though in slow-motion camera, he was able to see stark trees produce fresh clothing of green leaves, only to fuss like women of fashion, dyeing their dresses in various hues until they became brittle and fell away. So much of this went unseen to most people. All of it came pleasantly to the receptive eye of Arthur Bracegirdle.

The journey was in its closing stages as the train butted into the outskirts of Cotteston New Town and Arthur's face wore its customary frown as he beheld the messiness of the sprawling modern metropolis. The massive rows of concrete and glass factory buildings he found particularly displeasing. Custom built they might be, and efficient too, as the planners vowed, but in Arthur's opinion they were eyesores of the worst sort. Square and garish, they broke up the horizon like a buckled saw, their steam and air ducting reaching rocket-like into the sky.

Closer at hand, the intervening fields were a great deal easier to look at and he rested his eyes on their mottled green, moving his gaze slowly inwards till it fell on the shining, parallel rails of adjoining track. Here there was variety in the smoothly contoured embankment and the varied glimpses of hedges, dykes, allotments and tangled bushes growing beside the line. So much detail everywhere, all different and all whizzing through his field of vision like a wildly shaken kaleidoscope. Pylons and poles, cows and cart-tracks, seagulls and cawing rooks, thick spinneys and weed-covered ponds.

Suddenly, a tiny splash of bright crimson caught and held his glance. Here the track ran beside a public road and discarded along the route there was the usual conglomeration of litter and other objects. The spot of colour was an odd item though, and Arthur twisted his head to stay with the thing as it whipped away rearwards and out of sight.

And with practised eye, he identified the object.

Hell's bells! If he'd just seen what he thought he'd seen their must have been nasty work afoot. The glimpse had been fleeting and he might have been mistaken, but in his heart Arthur knew very well there was no mistake. His mind seethed, urging him into action. He glanced quickly at his watch. Well, there was a wait of ten minutes before his schedule called a halt and there wasn't much he could do till then.

But then. Then he'd have to do something.

CHAPTER 10

The man who first took the call at Cotteston Police Station was young, inexperienced and prone to fluster.

At eighteen and a half years old, Sam Hervey was a 'tweenie' too old to be a Cadet yet too young to be a fully-fledged policeman. Officially he was designated 'P.C' but under a local instruction he would perform only internal duties for the present, not venturing into the public eye until his nineteenth birthday.

Young policemen learn their job in the doing, and after a stint in the General Office, Hervey was in his first week of manning the switchboard. He was beginning to be good at it, fast memorising the various switches, so that he could route the more common calls almost without looking. But he was not yet good enough to be left alone.

Many calls arrive each day at a police station and among them there are a few which require prompt and expert attention. It would not be wise for a green incompetent to handle such a call unaided and Hervey had been briefed on the kind of calls to hand over. When he received an incoming call and heard somebody babbling about finding a body, he was glad to pass the call to an old hand, P.C Walter Grinton.

Wally Grinton had been a regular station-duty man at Cotteston Police Station for a lot of years and this was by no means the first call he'd handled that had to do with bodies. Calm and businesslike, he recorded all the details he could learn, pumping the caller for more and more facts, unwilling to break the connection until he felt sure there was nothing more to be had. Only then did Grinton move briskly from the switchboard and climb the stairs to speak personally to the C.I.D—always a better method of passing really important messages than through the telephone.

Matt Hollis was alone in his small office adjoining the main C.I.D room. He was working hard through a mounting back-log of paper but he had time to listen to Wally.

'Telephone call, Sarge,' the constable said. 'Re-directed from Piccadilly. Train-driver reports seeing a body near the track, or that's what he thinks it is.'

A sudden flash of interest in an otherwise dull morning. Hollis responded to it—asked questions.

'Is it on us?'

'Fair and square, so they reckon. About a mile south of the main road bridge on the Manchester line, lying in a ditch just off the track. If I know my stuff they must mean the big gully that runs beside Scorton Road.'

'What sort of body?'

'Now there you've got me. There isn't enough detail. He describes it as an arm in a red sleeve, sticking up out of the grass. You don't find many blokes in red coats, so I suppose it's got to be a female, but I wouldn't go firm on that. He didn't see the rest of the body.'

'It might be somebody sleeping rough, Wally?'

'It might be, but the driver says not. He says the arm was sticking in the air—and it never moved.'

'Does he, then? Well that sounds like a body, but we'd better have a shufti before we start ringing bells. See if Mr Wilson's in his office will you, mate.'

'He isn't. I can tell you that. He's in the canteen having a cuppa, or he was five minutes ago.'

'Dig him out will you, Wally? Ask him if he wants to come. Tell him I'm organising some transport and we'll be ready for off in a few minutes. Oh, and rough out everything you've got on a message pad, so we've got something to work on.'

Wally Grinton held out a sheet of paper covered with his own thin, neat writing.

'All yours, Sarge,' he grinned. 'Brought to you through the miracle of carbon paper.'

★ ★ ★ ★

At first glance it was hard to believe she was dead.

Her body was fully clothed and apart from a slight rucking of the skirt there was no disarrangement. Her nylon tights were badly laddered and plucked and one red wedge shoe had a broken strap, but the shoe was still in place on the small

116

foot. The girl looked peaceful, blooming, as though she had lain down in that spot to soak up the sun of summer.

Except that it was not summer and the sun was invisible beyond the clouds of a cold sky. Except that one arm stood stiffly out from the body, unnaturally still. Except that there was an area of flattened grass and herbage around the body and a wide strip, similarly flattened, formed a swathe from the body, up the rough bank and to the two-sleeper gap in the fence. And except for the pink stain of blood on the slack mouth and pale cheeks.

Wilson and Hollis approached carefully, making their own path in a roundabout route through undisturbed growth. Jim Wilson stood for a moment in doubt, then leaned and touched her face, hesitantly, as though she might feel his fingers and leap up in protest.

'Cold, Matt,' he announced. 'Not as chilly as store meat, but cold. We've a job all right.'

He picked up a stiffened wrist and probed without hope.

'No ambulance needed,' he went on. 'The surgeon can see this one where it lies. Nip away to the car, Matt, and get the usual stuff organised. You'd better speak to Mr Evans personally if you can. If not, leave a message for him to get in touch. Superintendent Naylor's off today, so tell Mr Shipley, he's acting-Super. I'll hang on here and see what there is to see.'

* * * *

Whereupon, like bees homing on a queen, the big guns of the County C.I.D, who were also the established experts in the technical investigation of major crime, came post haste to Cotteston to begin yet another murder hunt in a town that had seen more than its share of murders.

For Detective Chief Superintendent Evans it was the second homicide enquiry within a week. Four days earlier, the discovery of the body of a child in a remote part of the Ribble Valley had kept him from his bed twice round the clock, but the arrest of the child's mother had brought that matter to a satisfactory stage and he felt able, personally, to attend the Cotteston job.

A tall, lean man with close cropped grey hair and the wisdom of decades of experience hidden behind his plain, oval face, David Evans had been boss of the

County C.I.D for many years. He was nearing the end of his service and already the grape-vine was buzzing with rumours of his retirement, but about that he had said and would say nothing. He brought with him Detective Superintendent Ralph Challon, a seasoned detective who knew the Cotteston area well and who, after only a few months in charge of a District Task Force, had been appointed Evans' Deputy in the face of keen competition.

Challon's presence provided yet more fodder for the rumour-mongers. There was little doubt that one day he would take over Evans' role and the only unanswered question was how soon? But that was a mere side issue. For the present, Challon would be required to add polish to his own skill and experience by working in the shadow of the master, and that he was highly competent to do.

Evans arrived in his own official car with Challon as passenger. Other experts of lesser rank, from Headquarters, Scenes-of-Crime, from Photographic Branch, from Plan-drawing and from C.I.D Admin., made the journey in assorted transport, their equipment and their individual skills ready for use.

From the North Western Forensic Science Lab., came Evans' favourite team, Professor Arthur Harold Peterson, an eminently qualified pathologist known universally as 'Doc' and Doctor Frank Adams, an able forensic scientist and close friend. Peterson and Adams worked together as often as not. They had built up an effective three-way understanding between themselves and David Evans and would have been deeply hurt if Evans had failed to ask for them by name.

All these experts, aided by teams of less-experienced men from all branches of the force, began to take the scene apart in order to piece the story together, for the chain of circumstantial evidence so necessary to the detection of murder is invariably composed of many links—some so tiny as to be found only with difficulty.

The little-used strip of land between railway and road was roped off into suitable sections and a meticulous search carried out among the rank growth, the spindly trees and the assorted rubbish discarded by the good people of the district. A bewildering collection of matter—the relevant and the totally unconnected—was removed for more careful analysis elsewhere, in the hope that from much dross would emerge a few tiny nuggets of evidential gold.

The immediate surround with the body in situ was carefully screened from view and behind the screen Peterson and Adams performed their minor miracles of scientific detection. Police photographers exposed quantities of cine and still, fixing the scene from every possible angle and preserving a running record of what the eye might see at any stage of the search. And Frank Adams, himself a useful amateur photographer, took countless images of smaller but no less important detail.

Situated as it was beside a busy road, there was no way in which the scene could stay unnoticed. As always in such cases, the inquisitive public gathered in numbers to goggle and pry, gleaning their small share of the general excitement and offering good-natured resistance to the teams of uniformed men set to hold them at bay. Many officers were so employed. Good, useful men who might well have been put to more productive work. But their cordon task was important enough, for if a scene of crime is to yield all possible secrets, outside interference must be avoided at all costs.

Detective Chief Superintendent Evans hovered about the scene like an anxious mother-bird, dipping his fingers into every separate pie and constantly jollying his men along in case their efforts should flag. The local men, Wilson, Hollis and Detective Chief Inspector Murchison from Divisional Headquarters, organised the teams of workers, while Detective Chief Inspector Gerald Benson, Evans' Staff-officer, took personal charge of administrative matters, setting up and staffing Murder Control, laying on extra communications, procuring office equipment and organising reliefs and refreshments for everyone involved.

Much later, the body itself was removed, taken to the Town Mortuary, stripped and laid out on a porcelain slab for yet more photographing and examination before the final necessary indignity of post mortem surgery was performed.

As a routine matter, finger impressions were taken from the body for use in the vital process of establishing identity, of giving the victim a name.

But fingerprints have no voice of their own.

The expert can read their type, classify

the loops, whorls, islands, deltas, tented-arches and other points of comparison, but these details mean little in themselves. Only when set against other prints of known origin can they be used to show similarity or positive matching. Until that comparison is made, one fingerprint is very like another.

And because this woman carried no other evidence of personal details, the problem of identification was slow to unravel.

Peterson carried out the dissection of the body with his usual care. He passed on facts as they came to hand, but it was some time before he felt able to report the fuller picture. When he did so, the investigators were assembled in a small office set aside for Evans' use at a works canteen a quarter of a mile from the scene of the crime. This was the building Benson had acquired to house Murder Control, a set of rooms not in current use by its owners but which had many useful features adaptable to the needs of the enquiry. Here, checkers, clerks and filing staff kept a continuous record of events, including a detailed master-log of every message, every statement, every emerging fact in the progress of the case. And here Evans assembled with his inner cabinet of experts, to share views and express thoughts on everything that had developed so far.

Peterson was holding forth on his specialist subject, the structure and condition of the body, while the others listened in attentive silence.

'And so as to the time of death,' he was explaining, 'it strikes me as a wee bit unusual. I made the mistake of jumping to obvious conclusions. I began with the idea that the killing was done at night and that the body lay in the open right round the clock. But I checked the form and it didn't fit—so now I know it didn't happen that way. Give or take an hour, this young lady died only this morning, between six and eight, I'd say. You don't get too many killings at that hour, David.'

Wilson, the D.I, was only one of the listeners to prick up his ears at that particular item of intelligence, but he was the first to voice his thoughts.

'Stone me!' he said in surprise. 'We know who operates at that time. It looks like it could be our kinky handbag man.'

Taken off guard, Evans was slow to press for enlightenment, but only because his own memory had suddenly thrown up a fact that he'd already puzzled over.

'What handbag, Jim? She didn't have a handbag. And women without handbags are a rare breed. But this one was without, and that's a real puzzler if you ask me.'

★ ★ ★ ★

In the absence of direct evidence, some other means of naming the victim would have to be tried.

So a close-up photograph was obtained of the dead face, together with a description of the body and the clothing worn, and an 'Identify sought' notice prepared for distribution through the media. Once again the observant populace would be asked to lend assistance by studying the face and the details in press and on television. Because somebody was bound to know the woman. Close friends and relatives there might or might not be, but few people are completely anonymous to the world at large and it ought not to be long before somebody recognised the woman and rang in to say so.

As it transpired, the item was never used.

Because there *was* a handbag—and in

the late afternoon of that same day, the handbag was discovered.

The finder was a local man who trespassed on the main railway line, taking a short cut home as he had done for years past. He had little respect for the privacy of land but otherwise he was basically an honest man. Within ten minutes he had reported his find to the police—and within twenty minutes more, the handbag was lying on the desk in Evans' temporary office. It was a fat little bag in shiny red plastic. Its cheek was slashed open and its strap broken. Across its surface there were a number of dirty, greasy smears.

Using a local map, Jim Wilson was able to show Evans the spot where it had been found.

'More than a mile from the scene,' Evans commented. 'No wonder our search teams didn't find it. There's a lesson to be learned from that, Jim. We should have searched the line a hell of a sight further than we did, in both directions. In fact, it's not too late to cover that now. Get a team out to search that line from here to God knows where—and tell 'em to be careful of trains.'

'We damned near missed a trick there,' Wilson said.

'Yes. But never mind. We've got it now—and with those snapshots to compare there can't be any doubt that it belonged to the girl. We've got her name and pedigree.'

'Any thoughts on how it got so far away?' Wilson asked.

'Oh yes. It had to be a train, Jim. God knows how it got tangled and dragged along, but there's no other explanation. I'm more interested in how it got *on* the line, because I'm as sure as I can be that the woman was never further over than the ditch. We know exactly the route she followed—or was dragged. Doc Peterson found enough traces there to read it like a book.'

'It was thrown there, sir,' Wilson said confidently.

'How so?'

'Because it fits the pattern. That's the settled M.O of our unknown friend who's been doing these early morning assaults. On at least five of the earlier jobs he's snatched handbags and heaved them away round the nearest corner. We've said all along that he was after women and not

127

handbags, and this job proves us right with a vengeance. I'd say we're looking for the same man—acting in the same way.'

'And you've got some linked prints on these other jobs, haven't you, Jim?'

'That's right, sir. We've got prints, but nobody to tie them up with. He's a first timer. They've got nothing on him at L.C.R.O.'

'They will have before I've finished,' Evans said grimly.

'I want this bag dusted with pollen on an angel's wing. I can see marks there myself. If anybody smudges as much as a ridge I'll crucify the bugger.'

CHAPTER 11

Such a murder—or any murder for that matter—was bound to become known beyond the confines of the town, and since the press are notoriously better friends than enemies Evans followed his usual practice of calling a press conference within hours of discovery of the body.

Thus it was that a detailed account of

the incident was highlighted on the front pages of most newspapers on the following day, and the public thrilled to yet another spicy story of the taking of a young life with all its attendant overtones of sex and crime.

Sex where—in a technical sense at any rate—there was no sexual implication at all. In the words of the bulletin which was circulated later that day to all forces and whose main points were paraphrased by reporters for public consumption:-

'Her clothing had not been removed and there was no evidence of sexual interference.'

On the face of it, it was a senseless killing, for which the motive was not readily apparent. But privately, Evans and his colleagues had a shrewd understanding of the twisted minds and devious desires of the kind of men who carried out such deeds. Few crimes, and murder least of all, were ever completely motiveless.

The cause of death was not revealed in detail to the press, but in official reports it was described as *asphyxiation due to inhalation of blood and vomit.*

'Her own vomit, David,' Peterson was able to report to Evans, 'but quite obviously somebody else's blood.'

'The killer's blood, Doc?'

'It could hardly have come from anyone else. The girl herself didn't bleed at all, not in the normal sense that is. Of course, when human lungs are deprived of air to the point of collapse there's always a small amount of internal bleeding from ruptured cells, particularly in the brain, but that's no more than an effect which isn't manifested outside the body. No, the blood was from your killer all right. It probably led directly to the vomiting, and when the girl inhaled the mixture it clogged her air passages and she suffocated.'

'What caused him to bleed?'

'Her teeth. She bit his hand. There are pressure marks on the lips and cheeks that can only have been made by a hand pressed over her mouth for a long time. Her nostrils weren't covered and she'd be able to breathe that way until she eventually choked, but in the meantime she must have bitten him pretty badly.'

'So our friend's hand must be injured.'

'Undoubtedly. By the amount of blood and skin fragments on her teeth and face I'd say he has quite a few lacerations, some of them deep and nasty.'

'Bad enough for him to require treatment?'

'Very much so, professionally speaking. I'm not saying that he'll actually seek treatment, because people often leave the most dangerous wounds untreated—or treat them themselves—but if he's picked up the damage I think he has, any doctor would advise proper medication and dressing, and probably an injection as well.'

'We'll do the hospitals and the surgeries then, on the off chance that he turns up for treatment.'

'Oh yes, I'd say that's vital. Whether he turns up or not, it's an angle you can't afford to miss.'

★ ★ ★ ★

Climbing the flight of worn stone steps towards the entrance to the billiard hall, he self-consciously hid his injured right hand under the flap of his jacket, just as for long hours since the energy-sapping encounter he'd hidden himself from public view.

Like a fox fresh from a raid on the fowl-yard he'd gone to ground to sleep it off, his needs fulfilled for the moment, but when he'd wakened, refreshed in body, a little spark of insecurity had kept him indoors all afternoon. He'd even given the billiard hall a miss for once. But now it was the following day and he felt at a loose end. An hour with the clicking ivories was just the thing to restore his mood.

His hand still throbbed painfully, in spite of the soaking he'd given it in Dettol solution. He seemed to be carrying a handful of hot ashes. The self-applied pad and bandage was a rough, clumsy job that made it hellish difficult to hold a cue. Things might have been worse, though. If the bandaged hand had been his bridge hand, that would have buggered his game even more.

The place wasn't quite deserted, but there were few patrons in the hall on that gloomy November afternoon. Of the ten tables, only four were in use and there were no spare partners hanging about. If he wanted a game, he'd have to wait till somebody else came in. In the meantime, he took over one of the spare tables, trundling the gaily coloured balls about in a solitary practice session, feeding ten-penny pieces into the greedy meter whenever the lights failed.

With nothing much else to occupy his time lately, he'd got a fair bit of practice in, and as a result he was seeing the pockets better, handling the cue more expertly. These days he was good for a thirty break pretty often, and twice he'd topped fifty. A lot more of his shots were coming good, he noticed. In particular, he was squaring up to the difficult, cushion-run cuts into corner bags, and sinking them nine times out of ten. No doubt about it, he had a certain skill, and skills were things to make use of. With any luck, he'd hustle a few more bob from less-experienced players to add to the few quid he'd won already. He'd be back to give it another whirl tonight, when the end of day-shift brought its customary rush of new, green players.

But after a while he became bored with playing alone.

Far from improving his game, he found himself making more and more silly mistakes. Finally, after a more than usually poor shot, he flung the cue down on the green baize and stalked away from the table in a fit of sulks to find a seat on the side benches. The attendant saw the gesture and was less than pleased.

'Hey! Careful with them cues,' he shouted.

'Sorry. It was an accident.' A soft answer was best, because there was no point in getting the attendant riled.

'Accident be buggered. Them cues cost money.'

No response this time. Let the silly old sod have the last word. Meantime there was nothing to be done but sit and listen to the clicking, the cries of success and the disappointed oaths from other tables. Nothing but sit there and watch his own bought light burn itself away.

Ten minutes idleness and he needed a diversion.

He rose and walked to the attendant's small office and sweets kiosk where he picked up a copy of the Daily Express. Returning to his seat, he skimmed over the front page.

Another murder, the headlines told him, and a local one at that. Mildly interested he read through the account and was half-way down the second column before certain memory-nagging passages brought the message home to him. At first he only suspected, but when he checked the facts more carefully, noting place and time and circumstances, he knew with certainty that this was his own doing.

The truth hit him a blow in the ribs so hard that he dropped the newspaper in a loose tangle on the floor, climbed to unsteady legs and stumbled out of the hall, his thoughts racing and his face chalk white.

'Oh no!' he said aloud when there was no-one to hear. 'Oh weeping bloody Jesus, No!'

He'd never intended to kill the woman —couldn't believe that she could possibly be dead. The image of her motionless form was still printed on his memory, but he'd seen nothing in her stillness to suggest more than an ordinary fainting fit. It was such a crying bloody shame. She'd been warm and ripe and innocently young. The kind of woman a man might do many things to possess. But not kill. Not that, for God's sake. You didn't kill for it—ever. Nothing was worth that.

Once more he headed for home to hide his loathing.

Down the steps to the main street he was alone with his thoughts, but emerging into the chill of the afternoon he felt morbidly conscious of people around him—people who had eyes and whose eyes all seemed turned in his direction. But it was a passing illusion, and when he began to scrutinize the faces of passes-by he looked in vain for any spark of interest in himself. Why should they be interested anyway? They didn't know who he was or what he'd done. They couldn't have any notion how he tied in with the morning's news.

But after the first reaction to the news his attitude changed, and when the change came its speed and intensity surprised him. Half-way through town and moving towards home, his shock and disgust dwindled to be replaced by an entirely new, tingling sensation provoked by his wandering thoughts. It was a sensation of power.

The power of the living to bring about death.

It was easy to remember the woman, sensuous and strong. To feel her struggling and kicking in his arms but puny against his own power. He'd bent her to his will as easily as a stem of reed. She'd been like a writhing gardenworm to be held tightly between the fingers and crushed slowly, easily into nothing.

Christ Almighty! Had he really done that?

Had he squeezed the flame of existence from another human being as easily as shaking out a match? And was that special feeling of satisfaction something that always came with the ending of a life? He had never conceived of an outcome like that, but by God, in a funny way it had been good. And if he was capable of a thing like that, he could do anything.

Anything at all!

And next time, he'd do more. Sure as hell burned, he'd make the most of his chances next time. He'd been a brainless fool to have missed all those earlier chances, but he wouldn't miss any more. Next time, instead of stopping short at a cheap thrill he'd go all the way—really assuage that yearning hunger that the weakness of women created in his loins.

Something like that had been in his mind all the time, but he'd never realised until now that he really had the power to go through with it. Forgetful of the soreness in his hand, he flexed his muscles as he walked.

All of a sudden, he was impatient for that next time.

CHAPTER 12

Hetty Sephton (she'd been christened Henrietta but always did her best to avoid using that soppy name) sat in the interview room at Cotteston Police Station and moped. She was alone and feeling very put-out, angry almost, at having been dragged from her work right under the noses of all the office staff, bundled into a police car and brought here to see some chap who was big in the C.I.D.

This was the second time inside a couple of days that she'd sat unwillingly in this same room. It was coming to something when a body couldn't go about her own business without finding herself in and out of the police station like a common criminal.

The police lady, Miss Collinge, had told her it was something serious and then, on the way here in the car, she'd let it slip that they wanted to see her about the murder. Hetty knew about the murder because it had been in the paper that very day, and even though her conscience was clear she couldn't avoid being a little bit worried.

Not, of course, that they thought she'd had anything to do with the murder. That would have been quite ridiculous. But the Collinge woman had said they thought she could help. Well, in that case she really oughtn't to be cross. She didn't like people being killed, otherwise she'd never have agreed to come here at all, and on principle, if there was any way she could help the police to solve this one, she'd do it. Though for the life of her, she couldn't think how.

The man who came in with Miss Collinge was tall and thin, with soft brown eyes and a friendly smile. His hair was shiny grey, worn very short at the back and sides, and he had a grey moustache too, that was trimmed very close. Hetty warmed to the man even before he spoke to her at all. He seemed a very nice man. Some of her irritation eased, but not all of it. Before she calmed down properly, he'd have to convince her that this wasn't just a useless waste of her time.

Jenny Collinge smiled at her.

'This is Detective Chief Superintendent Evans, Mrs Sephton,' she said. 'He wants

139

to ask you a few questions about the murder.'

'All right. But it won't be the slightest use, because I don't know anything about it.'

The tall man drew a chair up to the table and sat facing her, quite close. He had a gravy stain on his tie, poor man.

'That's fair enough,' he said. 'We never thought for a minute you did. The fact is, Mrs Sephton, it's almost certainly a man we're looking for, a man who preys on women.'

'Why speak to me, then?' she asked bluntly.

'Because I think you know the man.'

She knew what he was driving at straight away and she wouldn't pretend to be surprised.

'Oh no, not that again. Look, mister, I've explained about that till I'm sick. I meet a chap for two minutes at a bus stop and you'd think I'd pinched the crown jewels. He was only larking about, I tell you, and no harm done. If that's all you want to talk about, I'm off home.'

She got up from her chair, but the detective ignored her and carried on speaking. She sat down again.

'I know how you feel,' he said, flashing another encouraging grin. 'Two days ago we accepted your account and let the matter drop, because, as you told us, there was no harm done to you. If nothing else had happened I wouldn't be raising it again—but something else *has* happened. Within twenty-four hours there was very serious harm done to another lady. She was killed.'

The look of sadness that crossed Hetty's face was genuine enough.

'Yes, and I'm very sorry for the poor girl, whoever she was. Her parents must be worried out of their minds. But I don't see...'

'The point is, Mrs Sephton, we think the same man might have been responsible—the man who was larking about with you the day before. That's why we think you can help.'

It was all absolute rubbish and she said so.

'You've got it all wrong. It couldn't be him. He's a very nice man. Not the sort who'd do any harm, I'm sure.'

'You may be right about that,' he said softly, 'but I've got to say I think you're wrong. In any case, I have to check up on him, and the only way I can do that is to find him and talk to him. Now you've already admitted you know him. Will you help me to find him?'

'No. I've already said I wouldn't. He's done no harm.'

He looked hard at her and his face was grave.

'Mrs Sephton,' he said heavily. 'Just suppose you're wrong and I'm right. We'll find out in the end, and then you'll be left realising you could have helped and didn't. And suppose, before we do catch him, he's killed some other poor woman. Would your conscience let you live with that?'

'What makes you so sure it's him?'

'I'll tell you. During the past two weeks we've had nine separate incidents reported of attacks on women, ten if we include yours. They all happened at bus stops, all early in the morning. The women were all waiting for early buses, just like you were, and all the attacks were similar. The latest one was the woman who was killed, and before that there'd been another woman who lost both her legs in an accident through running away from this man. Now that's serious, don't you think?'

'Yes but that doesn't make it the man I saw.'

'I think it does. I don't want to bore you with a lot of jargon, but we know that when a man commits more than one crime he very often sticks to the same pattern, the same *modus operandi* was we call it. If they find a way that seems to work, they keep on doing it the same way. So when we get a series of crimes like that, it makes us think the same person has done them all. Do you follow me so far?'

'I follow you all right, but this man didn't attack me. He was just messing about. Being silly. I didn't think that was a crime.'

'You're absolutely right, it isn't. But stealing handbags is. In all other cases the man either stole the woman's handbag or tried to. He had a go at yours too, if you remember.'

'But he wasn't trying to steal it. Definitely not.'

Evans could see why she was being difficult. She was still affected by a sense of loyalty to the man. He summoned patience and went on with his questioning

'But he knew you, Mrs Sephton. You knew each other. That would make all the difference. He knew that if he did anything serious to you, you could identify him. But suppose you'd been strangers to each other? You might have been in greater danger than you think. Don't you think that's possible?'

'No. At least, I don't think so.'

She wasn't playing yet, but she was beginning to waver. Evans pressed on hopefully.

'I'm asking you to think about it, that's all. Just one day after this thing happened to you, another woman was waiting at a bus stop early in the morning. She was on her way to work just like you. She never got to work, though. She was murdered.'

His blunt statement shook Hetty a bit, because it made some sort of sense. She still couldn't believe that the man at the bus stop—who'd danced with her, bought her drinks and robbed her of kisses—could possibly be involved in this other nasty business. But what if he was? What if this detective who painted a clear picture of some pretty awful happenings turned out to be right? Hetty shrank from the thought of getting the man into trouble for nothing. But if he deserved it...?

'What will you do if you find this man?'

'That depends on a lot of things, Mrs Sephton,' Evans said. 'If he turns out to be the man who killed this woman he'll be charged with murder, and if the court convict him of it, he'll probably go to prison for life.'

'And just supposing it isn't him?'

'If it isn't him, he'll go free. And you can rely on me to prove quite definitely one way or the other. It's easier to prove a man *didn't* commit an offence than to prove he did, and whatever you may have read in the papers, we don't charge people with things they haven't done.'

What he said sounded fair enough, and from the way he said it, Hetty was inclined to trust him.

'I'd like to help you,' she said, 'but I can't. I told this young lady all about him last time. It's years since I was ever in his company. I've seen him about the town plenty of times since, but I don't where he comes from or anything. Until that business at the bus stop I hadn't seen him for months.'

'Have you ever seen him there before?'

'At the bus stop you mean? No. Never.'

'And you use it all the time, don't you?'

'That's right. Every morning during the week.'

'Well just think about that, Mrs Sephton. Don't you think it's a bit strange that he should show up there on just one morning in all that time?'

She thought about it—and it did seem funny. Evans could see she was thinking and he pushed ahead.

'I'd like you to think hard, Mrs Sephton. You've known this man casually for a number of years. You must have heard him say something about himself—a nickname? Or the sort of job he does?'

'No, I don't think so. He was always a bit cagey like. I can't think that he ever mentioned a name, or not a proper one anyway.'

Evans noticed the qualification and pricked up his ears.

'Did he mention any name at all—proper or otherwise?'

'Well, yes and no. I remember asking him once. I kept on at him because I wanted to know, and in the end he said something silly. "Mickey Mouse" I think it was. I remember thinking he must be married and didn't want me to find out in case I told the wrong people.'

Mickey Mouse? A fine lot of bloody good that was. Evans concealed his disappointment.

'Speaking of names,' he said. 'What about the name you gave to Miss Collinge here? We've looked high and low for the man, but we can't find him.'

She wriggled in her chair uncomfortably, guiltily.

'I said he was a friend of his, didn't I. Well it's no good looking for him. I made him up. She kept pressing me to say who I'd seen the man with and I gave her a name just to shut her up.' She looked apologetically towards Jenny Collinge. 'I can't even remember what name I gave.'

'It was Harry Jenks,' Evans supplied.

'Well there's no such person, so you can stop looking.'

'All right,' Evans said blandly. 'We'll forget about that. But I want you to be quite clear about the main thing, Mrs Sephton. You may not realise it, but you're almost certainly covering up for a killer. Are you quite sure there's nothing else you can tell me about him?'

She began to cudgel her brains and Evans could see it happening. He waited, watching her narrowly.

'There was one thing,' she said eventually, 'but I... No. He must have been joking.'

'Joking or not, tell me what he said.'

Hetty didn't know if it would help, but she surprised herself by realising that she wanted to help.

'He didn't say it to me. He was talking to some other people at a dance. He'd been drinking a lot and he started talking about booking people for speeding.

'He said he used to be a traffic cop.'

CHAPTER 13

'Colin Duffy,' Wilson said. 'A pound to a pinch of shit.'

Wilson, the long-serving local man, had been Evans' first port of call with his new snippet of information. He was so gratified to have an immediate response to his query that he ignored the vulgarity.

'You know him, Jim?'

'I should say so, sir. He worked in this town for getting on five years. There's nowt you can tell me about Duffy.'

'But you can tell me, Jim. So let's have it.'

'Well, I've thought of a snag straight away. Young Frank Johnson knows him as well as I do. So if it really was Duffy, why didn't Johnson recognise him?'

'God knows. He might have changed a bit with age. What about the other chap, Hibbert?'

'Not Hibbert, possibly. He was before Hibbert's time. But I'd have thought Johnson would have known him. He's on duty now. Want me to have him in and pop the question?'

'Yes. I'll have a word with Johnson, but not straight away. Tell me about Duffy first, so I'll know what I'm talking about.'

'O.K sir, that's easy enough. Duffy was a good young copper in his day. A bit too keen for my liking, but it was his job to be keen, so I mustn't grumble. If anything moved, he booked it. He used to be at court damned near every session. Always traffic stuff, mind. I don't think he ever picked up a decent prisoner for crime in all the years I knew him.'

'He finished up in Traffic, didn't he?'

'That's right. It all worked out for Duffy,

because he got a transfer into Traffic pretty quickly, and that was where he wanted to be. Then, when he had about seven or eight years service, he resigned.'

'What the hell for?' Evans said, surprised.

'He had to. You know the score, sir. Ticket in as an alternative to dismissal. He'd got himself tied up with a policewoman and he was giving her plenty. To be fair though, they were both single at the time.'

Evans grinned broadly.

'Comes of having a mixed Force, Jim,' he joked. 'But that's not all, surely? Our girls don't take a vow of chastity.'

'That's right,' Wilson agreed. 'But when a bobby's working he's supposed to work. The bother in Duffy's case was that his girl-friend was stationed over in 'C' Division, a good twenty miles off Duffy's area. If he'd gone fixing her up on his Rest Days nobody would have given a damn, but it turned out he was across there when he should have been here—and complete with patrol car.'

Evans nodded.

'I've got the picture now, Jim. How did he fall?'

'As soft as you please,' Wilson told

him. 'Evidently he had her with him up a country lane, both of them supposed to be on duty but both well off their beats, and when he was turning to come home he backed into a wall and stove the boot in.'

This time, Evans' grin was sympathetic.

'Sod's Law says it always happens. Go on.'

'Well, if it had been just a scratch he'd have done the usual, got it touched up and kept his mouth shut, but you can't cover up fifty quid's worth of damage, so Duffy told lies about it. He hot-footed back here and then back-swiped another wall up in Old Cotteston, stayed at the scene and reported in that he'd had the accident there.'

'It's an old trick, Jim,' Evans said, 'and we'll never know how many times it's worked. Duffy might have got away with it.'

'He might have, but he didn't. It's a funny thing, but bobbies always seem to run short of luck whenever they try a fiddle.'

'Yes, I've noticed that. What happened?'

'Some bloke was walking his dog in the lane and they didn't know he was there. He saw the first bump, watched Duffy and his bird climb out and look at the damage—both in uniform, mind—and then watched them drive away. He took the car number and reported it. It didn't take us long to sort the job out then, and when Duffy could see the jig was up, he coughed the lot.'

'What about the woman?' Evans said quizzically. 'It sounds as though she must have been just as much to blame.'

'That's right. She was. And her ticket went in the same time as his. That way, there wasn't much publicity.'

'He wasn't charged, then?'

'With "due care"? No. The lane wasn't a road within the meaning of the act. He might have been done for damaging police property, but the real damage wasn't intentional. There was talk of a discipline job, but in the end he was given the option to go off, and he took it.'

'And now Duffy's back in Cotteston, is he?'

'Yes. They both are. He did the decent thing and married her. They've got three or four kids now, and they live in those old terraced houses off the lower end of Tower Road. I see them about now and then.'

'An ex-bobby,' Evans mused. 'Well, that would explain the uniform trousers wouldn't it? I suppose he'd have a few pairs left. How long is it since he put his ticket in?'

'Six or seven years. But I shouldn't think he's still wearing his old kit. He wouldn't need to, as it happens.'

'What makes you say that, Jim?'

'Friend Duffy's still in uniform. He has been more or less ever since he resigned. He's a security man at Justin and Peacock's the Metal-smelters up on Beech Bank.'

'That'll be shift work, won't it?'

'Yes, after a fashion, though I gather they do eighty percent nights. Just the odd week of days now and again.'

'Finishing about sixish, I suppose?'

'I'm not sure, but we can soon find out.'

Evans jutted a determined jaw.

'We're on to something, Jim. I can feel it. The more you talk, the more likely it looks that he's our man. He'll be knocking about regularly at the right sort of time. So let's have the bugger in.'

'What about Frank Johnson, though?' Wilson said. 'Shall we have a word with him first? See what he says?'

Evans considered for a long moment.

'No,' he said eventually. 'We can do that any time, so I'll keep Johnson up my sleeve. He might be an ace card. Get somebody onto it straight away, Jim, and parade Mister Duffy before me.'

'You'll want him at Murder Control?'

'No. He'll be happier here at the nick, where he can remember what things used to be like. I'll see him in your office.'

★ ★ ★ ★

The dead girl's name was Ellen Nuttall and she lived in a twelfth floor flat in one of the new high-rise blocks on Tower Road.

These facts were not known until her handbag had been found and handed in, but the contents of the bag, carefully and delicately removed to avoid destroying evidence were very revealing. Amongst them were letters written to the dead girl and photographs of her in solemn as well as in laughing mood. The photographs linked handbag to body and the letters yielded her name and address.

But identification is never complete until

there is proper testimony, and in most cases that is a problem for the next of kin.

By coincidence, just as Superintendent Challon was collating details and preparing to visit the flat to break the unhappy news to her family, the girl's mother called at the police station to report her daughter's failure to arrive home from work.

If anything, Mrs Nuttall's arrival made Challon's task the harder. Psychologically, the bearer of ill-tidings has a decided advantage if he can initiate the news rather than merely relate it by way of reply to questions from the recipient. But Challon was well used to handling unpleasant interviews of that kind. Firmly but courteously he broke the news—and afterwards cushioned the shock in the only way possible, by supplying hot tea and endless sympathy.

Which left him with the uncomfortable chore of leading the tearful and distraught woman through the distressing business of visiting the mortuary, viewing her daughter's body and afterwards supplying a long statement which, apart from setting seal on the matter of identity, also contained a wealth of personal details about the dead girl herself.

Ellen was nineteen years old, a waitress at a Motorway Services restaurant, and at the time of the attack on her she was en route to report for the morning shift. She was an only child. Her parents had been amicably divorced a few years earlier and Mr Nuttall had since remarried and gone to live in the London area, leaving Ellen and her mother to keep house together.

It took Challon several hours to extract these and many more facts from Mrs Nuttall, but the time was well spent. Apart from forming the mainstay of a report for the Coroner, the statement would also be useful as an aide memoire, when, as a matter of course, the victim's history, activities and known associates were minutely enquired into. Challon himself detailed and briefed the team of experienced detectives who would interview all her known contacts, including her father and her mother. Regardless of painful side effects on those involved, such interviews were vital. For, as Evans never tired of pointing out, the most likely first suspects in cases of murder are those who have some relationship with the victim. It was true that in the present case all available leads suggested an attacker who was unconnected with the girl or her circle of friends, but intuitive pointers are apt to mislead and all the routine stones had to be turned first.

There is always a harvest from well-husbanded enquiry.

The picture emerged with some clarity that Ellen Nuttall had been a decent, clean-living girl with no regular boyfriends and little tendency to make contacts outside her family circle. She had no known enemies and had always been on excellent terms with both her parents. As to her movements, she had used the same bus stop regularly over a long period and, until the last occasion, had always arrived promptly at work.

★ ★ ★ ★

When, one by one, her contacts were interviewed and eliminated from the list of suspects, Evans became certain that this time the initial pointers had not lied. He made the point as he sat in the Sub-divisional Superintendent's office at Cotteston, discussing the case with his friend and colleague, Superintendent Henry Naylor.

157

'There's no sordid family secret here, Henry,' he said, 'and I'm not in the least surprised. The bloke we're after is an ordinary nutter with a sex hang-up. He's found a new circumstance and a new time of day for his dirty little assaults and the Nuttall girl's death is just part of the pattern. Those ten jobs are all linked, I'll stake my life. A half-hearted bag-snatch on the one extreme and a murder on the other. All within a fortnight. Whoever our man is, he started small and worked up quickly to bigger things. Now he's gone as big as he can go, but he won't stop, Henry. Mark my words. Unless we get lucky and nab the bugger we could find ourselves with a string of really nasty jobs on our hands before long.'

Superintendent Naylor nodded his head in agreement.

'Looks like it, David,' he said. 'But to be honest, I think you're well off the beam with young Duffy. He's the wrong type altogether.'

'We'll soon find out, Henry. I've got the lads out looking for him now, and I might surprise you. You must have known him pretty well?'

'Oh yes, I knew him all right. And I'll

158

tell you this, David. If Duffy's involved in this in any way, it'll shake me bloody rigid. I used to have a good regard for Colin Duffy when he was serving. He was a good policeman. Given time, I think, he'd have climbed the tree a bit, and to be truthful I didn't like pushing him off the job. But there was nothing else for it, of course. Quite apart from his little masquerade with the car, he could never keep his cock in his trousers.'

'Neither can the bloke we're looking for,' Evans pointed out. But Naylor was not prepared to accept that. He screwed up his face in doubt.

'Come on, David,' he chided. 'You've got that all wrong, haven't you?'

'How's that, Henry?'

'Well, the rape bit's just what we *haven't* got. We've got murder—and there's nothing worse than that—but from what you've been telling me there's no evidence of a sex angle apart from the most crass amateur fumbling. The chap's feeling his oats all right, we both know that, and that's what's driving him. But I get the impression he's as green as grass. If he knows no better way of having it off than grabbing some strange woman in the street and whipping her skirts up—well—I don't give him many marks for wick-dipping.'

. Evans considered Naylor's point and found it logical.

'I suppose he *is* a bit like a little lad when you put it that way, but we know very well what he's after. His mind might be small, but his body certainly isn't. The way he dragged that girl through the grass makes him a powerful bugger for my money.'

'And yet he never got anywhere,' Naylor argued. 'He was strong enough to drag her through a fence and chuck her in a ditch, strong enough to throttle the life out of her if you like, but too bloody green to do anything more. You know what it says in the official report, David, because you wrote the bloody thing. She wasn't interfered with sexually.' He narrowed his eyes and stared suspiciously at Evans. 'Unless you buggers are keeping quiet about something?' he finished.

'Good God, no. It's a true bill, Henry. According to Doc Peterson he didn't even get as far as a hand up her knickers.'

'And you're blaming Duffy?' Naylor laughed loud and mockingly. 'Call off your hounds, David. Duffy could fix 'em up as soon as look at 'em. If Colin Duffy had dragged this girl into the ditch you'd have had a bloody sight different story to write. Besides, a chap like him wouldn't have to go fumbling round stray women at bus stops. If Duffy was going short, he'd fix himself up with something permanent among the local lasses.'

Evans felt bound to defend his views

'He did some fumbling at the bus stop in King Street a couple of days ago, remember. And that was Duffy all right. No bloody argument about that.'

'Maybe, David. But you're only proving my point. He knew the woman. She wasn't just a stray piece he happened to find there. And as soon as he recognised her, he started to tap her up. Now that's Duffy all over. If she'd nodded her head he'd have had her round the back of the Odeon with her pants off. But she didn't nod—and there was no question of dragging her away. Duffy wouldn't need to do any dragging. I reckon you're on the wrong horse, David.'

'You could be right, Henry, but I'll tell you better when I've had a bit of a go at Duffy. Give me half an hour with him and I'll come up with an answer—one way or the other.'

'You sound pretty confident about it.'

'Do I?' Evans grinned. 'That's because I *am* bloody confident, and I'll tell you why. You know we got prints off four separate handbags, including the one belonging to the dead girl? So far, the last ones haven't been properly matched up with the others—not in an evidential sense anyway—but unofficially, my lads tell me they're certainly the same man. So I've got his prints.'

'Duffy's prints?'

'I didn't say that. I don't know for certain whose they are. I'm just betting they're Duffy's'

'Are they complete, or only partials?'

'Oh, there's bags of detail, Henry. Enough to go through the index, anyway. But it looks as though our man's a first timer—not on record. So one of the first things I'll do when Duffy comes in is print him—whether he likes it or not—and I've Terry Milligan from Headquarters Fingerprints standing by. He can match them up for me on the spot.'

'Wait a minute, David,' Naylor interjected. 'Aren't you missing something? Duffy was a policeman. All policemen have their prints taken under the terms of the job. Won't

Duffy's still be on record?'

'You'd think so,' Evans agreed, 'but you'd be wrong. We haven't got them any more. It has something to do with civil liberties. When a man leaves the service, his prints are destroyed. That is,' he added with a sly nod, 'unless he left following a criminal conviction.'

'Which Duffy didn't.'

'No. But never mind, Henry, there's more. If Doc Peterson hasn't lost his touch—and that wouldn't happen in a month of Sundays—our friend should have some pretty hefty teeth marks on his hand. He gagged the woman with his hand and she chewed him up badly. Her lips and teeth were coated with blood and bits of skin, so that speaks for itself.'

'You'll have done the hospitals—and the doctors?'

'Naturally. We're doing them now, anyway. Ralph Challon has a team going round the lot. It's a long job, though, and if Duffy turns up with cuts on his hand we can short circuit Ralph's enquiries.'

'You reckon that'll clinch it?'

'I'm certain it will. In fact, if I *do* find those cuts, I'll boot Duffy into a cell without asking him any questions at all.'

CHAPTER 14

It took them a long time to find Duffy.

When Matt Hollis and D.C Jack Reade called at the house he was not at home and his wife, Della, treated their questions with open suspicion that was almost hostile.

'Where is he, Mrs Duffy?' Hollis asked politely.

'How should I know? I don't keep him on a lead.'

'How long has he been gone?'

'All morning. Since after breakfast.'

'When do you expect him back?'

'When he shows up. You should know Colin, Matt. Anyway, what do you want him for?'

Hollis couldn't duck the obvious question, but he'd been well briefed and he played it cagey.

'Routine enquiries, Mrs Duffy. You know the drill. We've been given a long list of people to check up on and Colin's on the list.'

'A long list, eh?' He could see her

thoughts turning over. 'So it's a big job, then?'

'Fairly big, yes.'

'Something wrong at the factory, is it?'

'No, not the factory.' It was impossible to lie.

'Well what is it then?'

'Oh come on, Mrs Duffy. I want to see Colin. You know I can't discuss it with you.'

But Della had done her calculations by now, and a strained looked appeared on her face.

'It's the murder, then. That's it, isn't it?'

'If you must know, yes.'

'Oh God! Don't tell me you think Colin killed that poor girl? You can't be serious. Colin wouldn't hurt a fly.'

'I didn't say we think he did it. We just want to ask him a few questions, that's all.'

'But you suspect him, don't you? Or you wouldn't be here.'

It seemed to Hollis that the time was appropriate for a well-chosen half-truth.

'He's a suspect, along with dozens of other people. You know what that means. It means we've got to go through the list, eliminating people, till we narrow the suspects down. But to do that we've got to ask a lot of questions and, just in case he's the right man, we've got to be suspicious of everybody. To that extent, we suspect Colin. If he's as harmless as you think he is, you've nothing to worry about. Now, for God's sake, Mrs Duffy, when do you expect him back?'

He was pleased to see that she seemed reassured. The worried look left her face and she smiled pertly.

'Why all this Mrs Duffy, Matt? It used to be 'Della' in the old days. You *have* got stand-offish since you got your stripes.'

'All right, Della, then,' he said, controlling his mounting irritation, 'but for God's sake, woman, this isn't a social call. I might be having to lock your husband up.'

She grinned.

'Not a chance, Matt. Ask him all the questions you like. It won't do you any good.'

'Where is he, then, for the third time of asking?'

'Off on the razzle with some of his boozing mates.'

'Is that what he said?'

'No, but it's where he is. Do you think I can't see straight through him? He's off work till tomorrow night and he's just drawn a bonus. He'll drink himself silly and I'll be lucky if I see him back before midnight.'

Matt Hollis studied her face. Della was plainly displeased about something, but if Hollis was any judge her displeasure was directed not against the police for chasing her husband, but at Duffy for playing away.

'I'll have to see him, Della,' he said. 'Will you give me a ring when he comes in?'

'Where from? We've no phone.'

'There's a kiosk at the end of the terrace.'

But Della wasn't ready to put herself out.

'No, damn it,' she said firmly. 'I'll tell him you called, but if you want him, you must come and get him.'

★ ★ ★ ★

They left the house, but they didn't move far away. Reade parked the C.I.D runabout on a croft along the street and they watched

Duffy's doorstep, determined to be on hand when he showed. He came home at five o'clock in the morning displaying all the night-worker's contempt for convention, coupled with the effects of a skinful of booze. In tones loud enough to wake the dead, he announced his intention of going nowhere—seeing nobody—but nevertheless, he went with them. At the police station they sat him in a cell to sober up while they roused Evans from his bed and told him certain things.

★ ★ ★ ★

The great man turned out without so much as a grumble and by seven o'clock he was facing Duffy across a desk in Detective Inspector Wilson's office.

'Show me your hands,' Evans ordered.

Duffy was far from sober still, but he was thinking rationally. He didn't like being where he was, and he'd give some bugger a right rousting about it before long. But the time for rebellion wasn't yet. Meekly he held out his hands.

Evans examined them with close attention, though with very little hope. He'd done his sums before coming to the interview and he knew very well, from Matt Hollis, that Duffy's hands showed no sign of serious wounding. But Evans was a persistent man, who would never let such a useful lead collapse till he'd personally killed it stone dead. Poring over the hard and calloused palms he found three separate cuts, all on the right hand. One was a clean incision, short and fine, but the other two might just have been punctures. Evans started to hope again, just a little.

'How did you come by these cuts?' he demanded.

But for Duffy, the thing had gone far enough.

'Mind your own bloody business,' he said. 'And while you're at it you can tell me what I'm doing here. I know the bloody rules, mister. I've got a right to be told.'

Evans fixed him with a blank stare.

'You've already been told, Mr Duffy. You were told by Detective Sergeant Hollis that I wanted to see you in connection with a murder. Isn't that so?'

'All right. He did say something like that, but I know nowt about a murder.'

'Be that as it may, you've been brought here to answer questions about it, and that's exactly what you were told. As an ex-copper, you'll know all about the ruling in *Christie v Leachinsky*, I've no doubt. But I know the case too, and I've complied with it. You've been brought here on reasonable suspicion of being concerned in the crime of murder and you knew that before you came here. Do you doubt my right to have you brought in?'

'Yes, I bloody do. You've got no evidence against me.'

'I've got reasonable suspicion, Mr Duffy. And that's all I need. *Reasonable suspicion.* That's what the book says.'

'But you're bloody mistaken. I've done nothing.'

Evans held out the offer of hope.

'All right then. Convince me of it. The sooner you do that, the sooner you walk out of here. Now I ask you again, Mr Duffy. How did you pick up those cuts?'

Duffy examined his own right hand. He was calmer now and the effects of drink were wearing off. He'd had his two-pennorth of grumble—made his point—and now he'd show this silly bugger how wrong he was.

'How the hell should I know?' he said, after locating and squinting at the cuts. 'Looks like barbed wire to me.'

'You done much climbing fences lately?' Evans asked sharply, trying to score a point.

'No. But I've done a hell of a lot of checking fences. Haven't they told you? I spend ten hours a night walking round fences and there's barbed wire all over the place. I'm bloody surprised there aren't more cuts.'

It was a very reasonable explanation and Evans knew it. In any case, even as a layman he knew very well that those few tiny cuts were not consistent with the kind of lacerated mess Doc Peterson had warned him to look for. But Evans never gave up on an interview till he'd wrung every drop of possibility from it. Even a man as efficient as Doc Peterson might have got it wrong. Suppose it wasn't a *hand* that had gagged the woman but some other part of the body? A forearm, for instance? Suppose that under the sleeve of that smart blue boozing suit there was a mass of torn, scabbing tissue? Sooner or later, he'd spring that one on Duffy, just to make sure. First, though, there was another matter he must be questioned about.

'Tell me what you know about Henrietta Sephton,' he said suddenly.

171

'Henrietta who?'

'Sephton. You heard what I said.'

'Who's that? The name means bugger all to me.'

But it did mean something. Evans could tell at once. At the first mention of the name, Duffy had lost some of his colour and a shadow crossed his face. The change was tiny, hardly noticeable, but Evans had spent a lifetime noticing such things. With the flair he had for choosing the right psychological moment, he raised his voice to a shout.

'You're a liar, Duffy,' he snapped. 'On Tuesday morning of this week—just three days ago—you were at a bus stop in King Street, on the corner of Market Street, at half past seven in the morning. Mrs Sephton was there too, and you molested her. Don't tell me it didn't happen, Duffy, because two of my men saw you—and one of them knows you well.'

It was the kind of shot for which Evans had become famous. Johnson had failed to recognise Duffy at the time and had said so. But *he knew Duffy from the past,* which was the only point Evans had sought to make. If Duffy chose to misconstrue, then so be it.

172

Duffy felt his resistance dwindling. This bloke asking the questions obviously knew what he was talking about and was not going to be put off easily. There certainly had been a couple of bobbies there at the time. He hadn't seen their faces—hadn't stayed long enough to look—but it was quite possible that one of them had recognised him. In any case, this bus stop job was bugger all, really. Not in the same street as murder. In his own wider interests, Duffy was ready to talk about a bit of canoodling.

'Oh, you mean Hetty,' he said, forcing a grin. 'You threw me, calling her Henrietta. Don't tell me that's her name?'

Evans relaxed and eyed his man with satisfaction. Having found the kind of response he was after he made ready to widen the crack in Duffy's defences. This part was going to be all downhill from now on. He'd got a straight cough from Duffy on one of the bus stop jobs and he still believed they were all linked. He considered his next question.

But he never got round to asking it.

At that stage, the door opened and Jack Reade poked his head inside.

'Sergeant Hollis wants to see you, sir,'

173

Reade said. 'It's something urgent. If you like, I'll watch this chap.'

Evans was reluctant to break away without delivering the kill, but he scented the importance of the message. Rising, he walked through to the charge office where he found Matt Hollis waiting.

'What is it, Matt?' he asked.

'We've just had another job, sir,' Hollis told him. 'Over on the Wingswood side. It happened about twenty minutes ago.'

CHAPTER 15

He exulted in the rediscovery of his power.

For the rest of the journey home he felt a new spring in his step and new plans chased themselves through his mind. The will to strike again had become a goad and the determination to make better use of his next victim was a strong force.

But during the next few hours, his enthusiasm waned.

For one thing, the dull pain in his hand seemed to be getting worse and he feared the onset of septic infection.

That scared him beyond measure and it also operated to deter him. Gradually he came to admit to himself that he could never face another morning sortie as long as the wounds continued to trouble him, even if that meant laying off for a very long time.

It took only a short night's sleep and a brand new idea to make him change his mind.

The idea came to him during sleep and he woke well before daylight with the details still sparking brightly in his head. Sliding quietly out of bed he stepped over the tangle of blankets and sleeping-bags that housed his younger brothers and sisters to where his clothes lay in an untidy heap beside the drunken wardrobe. He dressed quickly, accustomed to donning his clothes in the dark. Afterwards he rummaged gently in his junk-box under the bed, found the bottle he sought and slid it into his jacket pocket before easing out of the stale-smelling room and downstairs.

On his way to the front door he checked the alarm clock on the kitchen mantel. It wanted eight minutes for six o'clock. Ample time to move into position before the buses started.

Stepping out into the morning darkness he carefully drew the door into place behind him, listening for the click of the springlatch engaging. Then he stood stock still for a moment and gazed about him, thinking his way into the scene.

The street was lit, but poorly, a series of yellow balloons of light along both sides with great patches of shadow interspaced. The long double row of hazy patches seemed to stretch in both directions for ever, beside the endless rows of old-fashioned terrace houses. At first feel it was a fine morning, but in fact there was a spidery drizzle and he could see the droplets sparkling in the rays of the nearest lamp.

Two paces only, to the gate, and then he turned right, padding softly along the damp pavement. After only a few yards he hesitated, faced about and stood thinking. He'd started to head east, towards the town, by sheer force of habit. But there was no reason on earth why pickings shouldn't be just as easy towards the west, along the peripheral bus routes that weaved their way through the jungle of housing estates in that direction. Besides, with the last silly bitch dying on him there'd probably be hell on in the central district of Cotteston, and hitting the same area again might be too risky. He retraced his steps picking up speed as he went, continued past the dark front of his own house and onwards into untried territory.

When he reached the first estate his eyes became alive, reaching forward into the yellow blur of sodium lighting, picking out the bus stops well ahead on both sides, seeking the kind of situation necessary to his purpose.

He needed to find a woman alone —youngish too, if that were possible—but the second point was much the least important. And she had to be standing at some suitable spot, not too close to houses, yet close enough to some dark corner where he could tackle her without the risk of being seen.

In the course of the first half mile he found nothing that suited. At this hour there would have been more people about nearer the town and he began to rue the decision to transfer his attention to this deserted place. He passed a long series of empty stops and then came suddenly on a small group of women chattering and giggling at a farestage set back from the road. He eyed them as he went past. Any one of them would have been fine, but their plurality ruled out all of them. There was a lone figure two stops further on and he quickened his pace, feeling the onset of eagerness, but once more it was no use. The lone figure was youngish, but disappointingly male.

When a real chance offered, that too fizzled out.

The woman was in the right mould exactly and she stood at an isolated spot, but even as he moved in to make his play he was overtaken by the first early bus. He halted, chagrined and frowning, as the woman boarded the bus and was swept away out of his reach.

But there was plenty of time yet. He carried on walking, hunting, hoping. Along miles of footway and through several turnings he kept his hope alive, but there was nothing. Time was starting to run short now. Soon there would be more people on the move, and when that happened his chances would end until another morning.

And then he saw her.

She was a trim young blonde and she was not waiting at a bus stop at all, but standing in front of the lighted window of a grocery store, one of three isolated shops set on the very fringe of a sprawling mess of council dwellings. The nearest bus stop must have been thirty yards from her and for a moment he hesitated, wondering why she waited there. But what did it matter? There were no people or vehicles moving in the offing. Nothing to stay him.

The three shops were grouped in a mini-arcade with a half moon of flagged area in front of them, bordered at each end by low brick walls which jutted out towards the roadway like a pair of embracing arms. He moved in, to stand by the end of the nearest wall. From there he could see her clearly, but behind him there was deep shadow and against that background he felt safe from her eyes. It would only take a minute to drag her into the depths of that shadow, but after a moment's thought he abandoned that plan in favour of another, better place.

The main road was wide at that point and on the far side of it was a recreation ground. He knew the geography vaguely, having played there in his younger days, and he pictured an extensive area of grassland with a few swings and climbing-frames scattered about, a donation from the ratepayers towards the amusement of local kids. The gates to the park were directly opposite the shops and even at that distance he could see that they stood open. No problem of access, then. The set-up looked good. The boundary wall with its fringe of iron fencing was visible, but the darkness beyond the fence beckoned him. It was exactly the right sort of place for the purpose he had in mind, and once he pressed the girl through those gates he would have time to do anything at all in the safety of infinite darkness.

A brief check reassured him that the woman was still alone and the road deserted in both directions. The nearest houses were eighty yards away, and even if she managed to scream it was unlikely that the sound would reach that distance. In any case, the plan he'd worked out virtually assured him that she would not scream.

He was particularly pleased with the plan.

As a final check, he slid the small bottle out of his pocket and held it in his bandaged hand. The label on the bottle declared it to be Camp Coffee, but he knew it was nothing of the kind. He'd had the stuff in his junk-box for ages, ever since in a moment of bravado he'd nicked it from chemistry class and borne it home with no more purpose than to feel the thrill of successful theft. The bottle had been full once, but now it was less than full. That would be due to evaporation he supposed, but the loss was not important since there was ample liquid left. He'd never imagined it would prove useful, but now he'd found a use for it. A damned good use.

He had to have a pad, of course, but he'd thought about that. Didn't he carry his own pad? Wasn't the wadding of cotton wool and bandage dressing on his wounded hand as good as any pad? He unscrewed the metal cap from the bottle and soused a liberal amount of clear liquid all over the bandage. No time to replace the cap, and it didn't matter anyway. He placed bottle and cap carefully down beside the wall and then moved in.

Walking quietly, tensed, he approached to within a yard of the woman while she continued to browse through the window.

At the last moment, she turned towards

him, but by then he'd launched himself and the padded hand was searching for her face. With his free hand he circled her shoulders, gripping hard, and the fumbling padded hand struck against her nostrils and slid down to encompass her mouth. At the moment of contact she tried to scream, but he was too quick for her.

And yet there was a piercing scream.

It was his own.

★ ★ ★ ★

Pauline Rennie sensed the man's coming.

As usual, she'd been in a trance, filling that awful ten minute waiting time with fatuous dreams of a bright future for herself. How she, a mere receptionist-cum-filing clerk, could ever succeed in business, become a wealthy woman and marry a handsome but penniless drifter who scorned her wealth and wanted only her love, was not easy to see. But it was surprisingly easy to dream about, and Pauline had formed the habit of dreaming about it every morning between leaving her warm home and climbing into Mr Lacey's warm car. Usually she was dragged back to reality by the sound of the car approaching, but this morning she returned early to the real world.

Because she sensed the presence of the man.

Pauline turned in surprise and saw him looming over her, arms reaching to grab her. His hand struck against her face and amid the onset of fear she smelt a sickly, sweet odour.

She'd always known that if ever anyone attacked her she'd collapse in a horrid funk, and she knew she'd hate herself for being a coward. But it didn't happen that way.

At the instant of attack she half-opened her mouth to shout, and when the hand with its stifling pad slipped down over her nose and clamped across her mouth, a finger—the crooked little finger—popped in between her teeth.

She bit the finger as hard as she could.

She clamped her teeth together until they almost met, until she felt sure his hand would pull away and she'd be left with an inch long lump of dirty finger bleeding in her mouth. So she released the finger, prompted by the thought and the man's loud, satisfying scream.

'You mucky bugger,' she spat at him as

soon as her lips were free. 'I'll kill you, you dirty pig.'

And she might have done just that.

Because her dander was up and she hated him. She lifted a shapely, nylon-clad knee and drove it as hard as she could into the man's groin, feeling a solid thunk that hurt her own knee and must have done the man no good at all. She heard his long, grunting exhalation and felt a fierce sense of pleasure as he dropped to a crouch in front of her, groaning. But she could feel no pity for him.

In the stress of the moment, she mouthed unladylike curses and lashed out at him with her heavy wedge shoes, striking him on shin and thigh, ribs and elbow. She kept right on kicking, filled with an urgent need to avenge herself on this nasty man for his cowardly attack on her.

No horrid funk. Not even a spark of fear. In an odd way she felt proud of herself for having stood up to the attack so much better than she'd ever dreamed she would.

And then the man staggered to his feet and ran away from her at a shambling trot. For a yard or two she followed, still aiming kicks, but then she stood back and let him go, watching his departure with some satisfaction. He headed for the park gates and she watched him pass through into the dark nothingness beyond the street lights.

At that moment she became consciously aware of the sound of other running feet. But the new sound was loud, drumming. The attacker had heard the sound before she had, she supposed, which explained why he'd taken to his heels. Seconds after the attacker disappeared into the park another man came on the scene, running fast towards the park gates, to turn and disappear into the same darkness.

Pauline waited, intrigued, and after a few moments the newcomer returned, hurrying across the road to join her.

'He got away, I'm afraid,' he said. 'Are you all right, Miss?'

All right? She'd never felt better in her life. The lingering clouds of sleepiness had quite gone from her brain. She was warm with exertion, breathing like an athlete and ready to take on all comers.

'Yes. I'm all right.'

He was a very nice looking young man and obviously filled with concern for her safety. Pauline liked him.

'I'd have had him if I'd been a minute sooner,' he said.

'Well, thanks for trying, anyway.'

She felt a strange looseness about her right foot and looked down.

'Oh God! I've split my shoe.'

'Let's have a look at it.'

He knelt and took hold of the shoe, pressing the broken parts together. Pauline found herself looking at the crown of his head. His hair was brown, neat and tidy.

'It's no good, I'm afraid,' he announced. 'A shoemaker might fix it, but even if I had the tools I could only do a botch job. How did it get broken?'

'He banged his shins against it,' she said, 'as many times as I could manage.'

Pauline grinned happily.

The young man smiled in return, sharing her happiness.

★ ★ ★ ★

The ordeal of the interview that followed was greatly eased for Pauline Rennie. The young man, whose name was David something, refused to leave her until the whole thing was over. He insisted on going with her to the police station, fussed around

186

while they badgered her with questions, took her arm and led her outside, ordered a taxi and swept her home in style.

He was extremely courteous.

Even right at the end, when he was leaving and would soon be gone for ever from her life, he was courteous. And when, at the very last minute, he asked Pauline if he could please come and see her again, he said it very politely.

And he had lovely, misty eyes.

★ ★ ★ ★

He'd heard the running feet all right.

The sound filled his head, but his eyes had forsaken him and were sending no messages. Still, the runner was not close enough to reach him yet. He grunted with relief as he passed between the iron gates and away into a dark unseen world of springy turf.

But he needed to keep running. The hurt finger burned like fire under its thin coat of gauze and in uncaring agony he wrenched at the bandage as he ran, ripping the thing away and flinging it from him into the darkness. Then he slipped the finger into his mouth and eased it with gentle tongue, gasping and licking as he ran.

Somewhere beyond the expanse of grass he came to another line of railings with spiked tops. The spikes held no fears for him now. He hurled himself over them and fell heavily on the far side. Rising, he set off running again, all sense of direction gone. His staggering feet sank into soft ooze and thereafter, every pace was a straining, sucking labour. After twenty paces he could go no further, but at least he felt safer now.

He collapsed into the slimy mud and sobbed.

CHAPTER 16

Colin Duffy was released.

Contrary to a belief popular in some circles, the police cannot afford to waste time making things difficult for innocent men. Convicting the guilty takes time enough.

The new incident, just reported, was not conclusive in itself, for 'copycat' crime is a surprisingly common occurrence, but Evans had studied such evidence as there was against Duffy, and his professional instinct warned him that it had dwindled to almost nothing.

Certainly he was cleared of the murder, as Evans saw it. The relatively uninjured state of Duffy's hands was evidence of that—and the new incident served as a clincher. And since, at heart, Evans was only concerned with the murder, he was happy to let matters lie.

In turning Duffy out, Evans was completely frank.

'I won't detain you any longer, Mr Duffy,' he said. 'I had you tabbed as a possible killer but now I'm satisfied that I was wrong.'

Duffy was surprised when the interview ended so abruptly, but there was no gratitude in him.

'It's a bloody nice thing,' he said, 'being accused of murder when you're as innocent as a new lamb. You needn't think you've heard the last of this. I reckon I'm entitled to a proper explanation.'

'So do I, to be honest,' Evans said. 'Ordinarily I wouldn't say much more at this stage, but being an ex-copper you'll know how these things happen, so in fairness I'll give you the full picture. When I had you brought here, I already knew about that little adventure of yours with Mrs Sephton, but that was the least of my worries. As you'll be well aware, I wouldn't normally chase about after little things like that.'

'No. You just used it as an excuse to get me inside.'

'Come on now, you know that isn't true. You've been told no lies about it. You were told about the murder right from the start. I kept the Mrs Sephton job up my sleeve.'

'But that was all you had on me. There was nothing else.'

'Quite right, but as it happens we've had a string of attacks on women in the past fortnight and they all happened at bus stops early in the day. That's exactly how the murder happened. Same time, same circumstances. Same M.O if you haven't forgotten our technical jargon.'

'But I had nowt to do with it,' Duffy grumbled.

'I know that now, but I didn't know it then. I knew that whoever did those other little jobs also did the killing. The mistake I made was in thinking that the Mrs Sephton incident was part of the same sequence, and you've got to admit there were a lot of similarities. Since then, within the last half hour in fact, I've had information that convinces me I was wrong. I can't tell you what it is, but I can tell you it clears you of the murder, so you're free to go.'

'You got the wrong bloke, eh?' Duffy said unsmiling.

'That's the size of it. It isn't the first time it's happened and it won't be the last.'

'So this is where I see a solicitor and go for damages.'

Evans gave him a scornful look.

'You must do what you think best,' he said. 'I'm always ready to answer for the things I do. You can make an official complaint about it, too, if you wish. Just call at the public counter and they'll give you a leaflet. Believe me, it'll be properly enquired into—and by somebody of higher rank than me.'

Duffy scowled. He felt disgruntled about the whole rotten business but he didn't really feel like complaining. There was enough of the policeman left in him to remind him of the general uselessness of complaining. He'd been the subject of complaint himself, more than once, and knew the feeling at first hand. Lazy policemen who never did a stroke were never complained against—only the ones who were trying to do their job. Evans had been doing just that. He had shown no personal malice against Duffy. So what the hell...? He grinned sheepishly.

'O.K I was only kidding. But what about this other business with Hetty Sephton? Am I clear on that?'

'She doesn't want to make a formal complaint,' Evans said. 'She didn't object to what you did. Mind you, I'm not saying you were right to do it. If she *had* objected I'd have given you a run on the strength of what my men saw.'

'But she didn't—and you won't?'

'That's right.'

'In that case, I'll bid you good morning,' Duffy said.

★ ★ ★ ★

When Duffy went, Evans went too. But only as a courtesy.

Duffy walked out of the office with

Evans as a trailing escort. A former worker in that same building he knew the lay-out well enough and instead of taking the public route along the main corridor and through the charge office he turned right and took the short cut through the main C.I.D office. Evans was faintly amused and made no attempt to stop him. But as he was passing the first desk, Duffy stopped and looked down. Evans halted too, and watched with mounting interest.

There was a single poster lying on the desk. It bore the picture of a man and beneath the picture a description. Duffy turned to face Evans and pointed at the poster.

'A photo-fit eh?' He commented. 'Can I have a look?'

Evans was inclined to refuse, but thought better of it. He joined Duffy and stared at the picture.

'It's not a photo-fit,' he said, 'it's an artist's impression. We find they're better sometimes. But have a gander if you wish. It'll be public soon enough. As soon as it's printed there'll be one pinned on the notice board.'

'Is it your murderer?'

'As a matter of fact, yes.'

Duffy seemed inordinately interested in the poster. He studied it carefully for some minutes while Evans waited. When he looked up, he said:-

'I'd try the billiard hall if I were you.'

'What makes you say that?'

'I've seen that bloke before, or someone like him. He's a bit of a lone bird—only eighteen or nineteen but a big powerful lad. He hangs about the billiard hall sometimes, doing a bit of sharking with the beginners.'

'Tell me about him,' Evans invited.

'That's as much as I know.' Duffy said. 'I've never spoken to the lad, but he's a dead ringer for that picture. Try asking the attendant bloke. He'll know him for sure.'

'I'll do that,' Evans said shortly, 'and thanks.'

'One good turn deserves another,' Duffy said sarcastically.

★ ★ ★ ★

After Duffy had gone on his way, Evans mulled over the gratuitous tip in his mind. Could there be anything in it? He wasn't particularly hopeful.

The biggest drawback to the use of artists' impressions of wanted men was the fact that they were so general, giving no more than a rough suggestion of the man they were intended to represent. Evans looked hard at the latest in the line and to him it seemed a very woolly picture. It had been prepared carefully and patiently from details supplied by a number of witnesses, but in the end its quality would depend as much on the witnesses' memory as on the artist's skill. It was better than no picture at all, as Evans knew, but spot identifications made from it—like the one Duffy had just made—were bound to be suspect from the outset, and he'd need to be careful how he used them.

But it was a possible lead and he couldn't ignore it.

From Wilson's office, he rang Ralph Challon at Murder Control and passed the snippet on. Challon was as sceptical as Evans, but he arranged for Detective Constable Henderson from a stand-by squad to follow up the line.

Henderson was a competent man but no less dubious than his betters. He tackled the job with plenty of enthusiasm, but with the thought ever in his mind that it was probably no more than just another false trail.

★ ★ ★ ★

The attack on Pauline Rennie was investigated as thoroughly as if it had been a murder.

In a way, as Evans pointed out, it *was* a murder. Or at least it was an attack by an established murderer, in circumstances that could easily have led to death.

Police dogs and their handlers were quickly on the scene and in no time at all they ran a trail across the grass, pin-pointed the spot where the attacker had climbed out of the park and found the beginnings of a line of footprints leading across marshy bog. The whole area of land beyond the recreation ground was pitted with pond, marsh and ditch, but nevertheless Sergeant Phillips was convinced that his alsatian 'Briny' had run a true trail as far as the main Manchester road.

From that point, traffic fumes and the criss-crossed trails of many other people combined to put an end to that particular chase. Phillips tracked and retracked, but no amount of persistence could take him further.

When the dogs had had their day, the whole area of shops and recreation ground was thoroughly searched, and whilst the searching was going on, other teams of men went 'on the knocker' at houses in the vicinity, hoping to discover some early riser who might have seen or heard something.

By four o'clock that afternoon, a great deal of work had been done. Many more enquiries were still to be made but the case was progressing and Evans saw fit to hold court once more in his small office at Murder Control.

He had his team of experts gathered about him. Professor Peterson and Doctor Frank Adams were there, as were Detective Superintendent Challon, Detective Inspector Wilson and Detective Sergeant Matt Hollis. All were seated on hard backed chairs around a blanket covered trestle table and on the table were an assortment of items collected as evidence from the scene. These included a plastercast of a footprint, a crumpled bandage stained with blood and other matter and a Camp Coffee bottle with separate metal cap. The bottle carried a fine coat of light-coloured dust.

'It's the same bloke all right,' Evans commented. 'The prints on the bottle tell us that. We'll have to do a proper comparison of course, but Terry Milligan's had a look and he assures me the prints are the same as those we've got from the other cases. So if we clear this one, we clear the lot, and that includes the murder. Anyone got any ideas?'

As usual, Peterson was full of ideas.

'The man's getting ambitious, very fast,' he said. 'A fortnight ago he was playing about with women in the most mild, fumbling fashion, but since then he's killed one. He must know he killed her, yet he's still chancing his arm.'

'He damned near killed another woman, right at the start,' Evans pointed out.

'The woman who lost her legs? Yes, I haven't forgotten that, David. But all he did there was pick a woman who panicked. What happened after she ran was an accident, no matter how morally responsible he might be. Mind you, I'm still of the opinion that the killing was unintentional too, but that will be something for the court to decide, if you ever manage to bring a charge.'

Evans looked grave.

'I must be getting old, Doc,' he said. 'Time was, when all I cared about was clearing the crime, but in this case I couldn't give a blind toss about that. I want to catch the bastard just as badly, but my main concern is stopping his capers before some other poor woman goes the same way.'

'That's known as getting your priorities right, David,' Peterson said, 'and you've good cause to think that way. Because if this latest girl had died it would have been no accident. This chloroform business worries me. I know it's popularly believed to be safe in use, but in fact it can be lethal in quantity—and there was a copious amount used here.'

'It did her no harm as it happens.'

'No. Because she was too damned good for him. But I hate to think what might have happened if she'd gone under, as she could easily have done. She showed a lot of guts, that girl, and guts gave her the measure of our friend.'

'It's a pity she didn't grab him and hang on,' Challon said, 'because she could have done it, I reckon. But what about that chloroform? Where would he get it?'

'Hard to say, Ralph,' Peterson admitted. 'It isn't used half so widely these days as it used to be. Anaesthetics have advanced a bit in recent years. There are still a few industrial processes that call for it—and all sorts of chemistry labs still have some hanging around. But he won't have bought it—you can be pretty certain of that. He'll have stolen it from somewhere.'

'It would be handy to know where,' Challon said.

As usual, Evans was philosophical.

'It would, Ralph, but no matter. With a bit of luck we'll have him in before long and he can tell us himself. The bandage interests me more just now. You've run the rule over it, Doc. What do you make of it?'

'I'm still working on it, David. There are all sorts of tests to be done yet. But it's an eloquent bit of rag. I can tell you quite a lot just from looking at it.'

'Go on. Like what?'

'Well, for one thing it links him with the murder. That's assuming that it came from your recent attacker, but with the bloodstains and the chloroform all over it there can't really be much doubt.' He prodded the bandage with a pencil, raking through the folds. 'The staining confirms what I said before. You can see there are at least a dozen different seats of bleeding, small wounds but a goodish number of them. It doesn't take an expert to see that whoever wore that bandage had a badly mauled hand. I can't absolutely swear that they're tooth-wounds, but the general lay-out suggests it very strongly. And since the likeliest way of picking up that kind of wound is from biting I'd say it was Chester Cup odds that same hand caused the death of that other young lady, Miss Nuttall. For what it's worth, I can also say that the bandage is a self-applied job, roughly bound and inexpertly tied. On the other hand, it is a properly manufactured dressing.'

'A hand injured like that would be painful, wouldn't it, Doc?'

'Almost certainly. And I must say I'm surprised that he should use the same hand for the same sort of purpose so soon afterwards. Once bitten—twice shy, they say. But it didn't work that way this time. The poor sod didn't learn the first lesson, so he got bitten twice.'

'And right afterwards, he rips the

bandage off and chucks it away. Why did he do that?'

'That's something I can't answer. But by then he'd used it, which is why we find it soaked in chloroform. He'd obviously heard the old tales about putting girls to sleep with a stupefying drug long enough to have his wicked way, and he was crafty enough to realise that his bandaged hand would serve in lieu of a pad. This latest girl was damned lucky, David, when you think about it. If he'd taken her completely by surprise his scheme might have worked. You don't have to block people's mouths and noses for very long before they go unconscious—or worse. It isn't so much the drug as deprivation of air. We would all die very quickly if we didn't have air.'

'And if that happened, cause of death would have been more or less the same as in the other case?'

'Yes. But thank God he never had a chance with this young lady. She got a grip on his finger and that stopped him covering her mouth. And from what she tells us, it must have made a mess of his finger too. He's accident prone, this mauler of yours.'

'So we go all out for the damaged hand,'

Evans said. 'Mind you, if he treated his own injuries the first time there's little doubt he'll do the same again, which explains why your men had no luck at the hospitals, Ralph.'

'Another wild goose chase you landed me with,' Challon grinned. 'But there's a credit side too. It's bound to be useful for sorting suspects out. If we pick up the right bloke he'll have 'guilt' written all over his scars.'

Evans nodded in agreement.

'As a point of interest, Doc,' he enquired, 'could you match up that bandage with the hand it came from? The pattern of marks?'

'I'd had a damned good stab at it, David. Let me put it this way—I might not be able to convince a jury on just that one point, but I could sure as hell satisfy you.'

'And that's all I need,' Evans said grimly. 'If you can give me that much I can do the rest myself.' He turned to face Wilson. 'Now what about this witness, Jim? The young chap who came on the scene and saw matey scuttling off. He must have a good idea what he looks like?'

But before the D.I could answer, Frank

Adams interposed.

'Is that all you want from the bandage, David?'

Evans rose from the chair and sat looking down on the bowed heads of Adams and Peterson. His look was a mixture of doubt and awakening understanding. There had been something about Adams' question—its timing, perhaps—that put Evans on his guard.

The buggers were pulling his leg—he could read the signs. For all the good support he'd had from these two solemn-looking experts over the years, he'd never been able to cure them of having their little joke. They seemed to get a lot of sadistic pleasure out of needling him—and they were needling him now.

'My poor old mother, bless her memory,' he said with a pronounced snort. 'She warned me about crafty sods like you. She used to say, *if ever you catch a weasel asleep, pee in its earhole.* Pee away, if you think I'm sleeping.'

Adams raised his head and regarded him innocently.

'I'm not with you, David. What's that supposed to mean?'

'It means I'm never bloody satisfied with

what I get from you two. I'm missing something, aren't I? But the fun's over, Frank, so let's be having what you've got up your sleeves.'

'It's only a small thing,' Adams said, grinning widely. 'Not worth bothering about, really.'

'Let me be the judge of that,' Evans said heavily.

'Oh, all right, then.'

With a gesture of resignation, Adams used the tip of his pencil to close the bandage and turn it half way round. On the side that now faced Evans there was a tiny smudge of blue. Adams said nothing, but touched the bright colour with the tip of his pencil. Evans stooped to peer at it.

'What the hell is that, Frank?'

'Billiard chalk,' Adams said.

CHAPTER 17

By an accident of timing, D.C Henderson was at that moment reporting back from his uncompleted enquiries at the billiard hall.

Henderson had visited the place three times since lunch. The attendant had confirmed Duffy's tip in a loose way. There was indeed a youth who fitted the description and the attendant seemed to recall that he'd seen him recently with a bandaged hand, but he was unaware of his name or any other useful details.

'No bother, though,' he'd told Henderson. 'If you hang about you'll be able to ask him yourself. He's always here in the afternoon. Hardly ever misses.'

So Henderson had spent as much time there as he could spare but it had been unavailing. By four o'clock there'd been no sign of the youth and Henderson returned to Murder Control to report his lack of progress.

Evans was cock-a-hoop.

'It's beginning to tie together lads,' he said cheerfully. 'We know he goes snookering. There must be a lot of clubs with their own tables, but the billiard hall must be a good bet. And from what you've picked up, Henderson, this lad fits the description and also has a bandaged hand.'

'I don't think he was certain about the bandage, sir.'

'Maybe not, but we have to bank on it. It adds up to a full house near enough, and even if it doesn't, we're having the bugger in. I want somebody haunting that place till he shows up, and I want that lad bringing here.'

'He won't be in today, sir,' Henderson said. 'The attendant reckons he's never as late as this.'

'What time do they shut up shop?'

'About ten o'clock, most nights.'

'That's it, then. I want the place watching till it closes, and then I want somebody back there tomorrow, all bloody day if necessary.'

'I'll get straight back, sir,' Henderson offered.

But Evans had other ideas.

'No thanks, son. No offence intended, but it's not just a routine matter any more.' He turned to Wilson. 'You'd better take over, Jim. We don't want to go mob-handed or we might flush him too early, but you'd better have some support standing by. Take Matt Hollis, and young Henderson as well, since he started it off. Make sure you've got radios with you—and you two keep well clear unless Mr Wilson calls you in.'

★ ★ ★ ★

The finger wasn't as badly damaged as he'd thought.

There was a nasty, ragged cut on the soft pad under the second joint and a corresponding purple abrasion on the knuckle. The entire digit was beginning to puff up and it hurt like hell, but at least he could bend it and there was feeling right out to the tip—so it would mend.

The rest of his body was aching too, and there would be bruises in no time. She'd hacked him about a lot with her flying feet and he could feel the evidence on his ribs, his shins, his shoulders. Well, at least he'd managed to keep her from marking his face.

The earlier wounds in his palms were less angry and had started to scab up. There didn't seem to be any infection. To be on the safe side, he soaked the whole hand in Dettol but he bandaged only the little finger. He felt a lot better when he'd done that, and when he went to bed to catch up on sleep he stayed there longer than usual. It was four o'clock in the afternoon before he stirred himself to go for a game of snooker.

Late or not, the billiard hall was completely deserted and he could have his pick of tables. He made his way to the nearest cue-rack and selected the best he could find, rolling it on the flat of the first table to test for straightness. He decided to stay there. One table was no better or worse than any other.

He was a bit surprised when the attendant, a thin, consumptive-looking man with bottle lensed spectacles, left his cubicle and came over to chat. It was an entirely unusual show of interest.

'Let's see your hand,' the attendant said pleasantly.

Startled, he looked up from his cue-rolling and by reflex action shoved his right hand behind his back. The attendant raised his eyebrows, his face filled with open curiosity. He felt his own face grow warm with colour as he slowly brought the hand back to view, holding it loose-wristed.

'You had a bandage on it yesterday,' the attendant accused. 'I saw you.'

'What of it? I've still got a bandage on.'

He held the hand high, the bandaged little finger standing proud and the remainder clenched over his palm. The attendant looked and scoffed.

'Yesterday it was a big bandage. The whole hand.'

'Balls. You want your bloody eyes tested.'

He turned back to the table and began to fumble reds and colours from the pockets. The attendant stood watching as he stuffed the triangle, placed it, lifted it clear and palmed the pink. Then the attendant spoke again.

'What's your name, son?'

He looked up—eyed the attendant warily.

'What's yours?'

'I was only asking. I seen you in here a lot just lately. You live in these parts?'

'Sure.'

'I thought you must. Where abouts exactly?'

Why all these questions all of a sudden? The attendant had hardly said a word all these months and now he was quizzing like mad. The cunning old bugger wouldn't be doing it if he didn't have reason. Why did he suddenly want to know? His temper began to get the better of him.

'What's it to you, for Christ's sake?' he snapped.

The attendance shrugged his shoulders. 'All right, kid. No need to get shirty. Can't you speak to nobody without flying off the handle?'

'Listen, you,' he said grimly. 'I only come in this dump for a quiet knock-about, not to tell you my bloody life story. Never you mind who I am or where I come from. It's got sod-all to do with you.'

'O.K. O.K. Just trying to help, that's all.'

Help? How could he help? The attendant had given up and was walking away but he followed and took hold of the man by the shoulder, a thin, bony shoulder that seemed to shrink away as he gripped it.

'Just a minute, you nosy old bugger. You can't say things like that and then just calmly piss off. What's this about helping?'

The man turned his head. He had paled a little, but his grin was full of message.

'There was a bloke in here not half an hour ago, asking after you. I told him you was usually in before this, but you hadn't shown up.'

'What did he want?'

'Wanted to know who you was and all that.'

'Did he say who he was?'

'I know who he was.'

'Well, who was he then, you silly old sod?'

'He was one of the jacks,' the attendant leered. 'You been a bad boy, I reckon.'

The information rocked him on his heels. He was suddenly consumed with anger and with flying sparks of fear. He smothered the fear, but the anger bubbled over.

'And you was going to tell him was you, you sneaky little bastard? That's why you got so bloody nosy all of a sudden, isn't it?' He raised a doubled fist threateningly.

'I've a good mind to leather you, old man—teach you to mind your own bloody business.'

The man trembled under his hand.

'Come off it, son. I was just joking.'

'Joking, eh? You mean there wasn't a jack?'

'Oh no, there was a jack all right. But if you've done nothing, you've nothing to bother about.'

He pushed the man, sent him sprawling, but that was the last manifestation of his anger. Fear took over as the dominant emotion in his wildly fleeting thoughts. If it was right that a detective had been here, looking for him, asking questions about him, it was ominous. They must have got him taped some way—for something. Impossible to know what they'd found out about him, or what they suspected, but whatever it was they'd keep looking. It was a stroke of luck that the detective had gone away, but he'd certainly be back, and it would never do for them to find him here.

Trembling now, he walked to the cue-rack and flung his cue against it, oblivious of the clatter as it teetered and fell to the floor. Then he stalked out of the hall, firing his last shot as he passed the attendant.

'You want to keep your bloody nose out of other people's business, or somebody'll chop the bugger off.'

He quickened his steps as he moved through the exit door. By the time he reached the middle step, he was running.

* * * *

Fifteen minutes later, Detective Inspector Jim Wilson climbed up the same steps and walked into a livelier scene.

Three tables were now in use, two doubles and a fourhand, and another patron waited on a side seat, following play with critical eyes.

Wilson propped himself against the counter, took a packet of cigarettes from his pocket, extracted one and lit up. He blew smoke contemplatively and examined all the players one by one, looking for bandaged hands. None.

He waited till he caught the attendant's eye, then he winked and jerked his head. He walked into the gloomy corner beside the kiosk and after a minute the attendant followed. The busy patrons paid no heed. Wilson grunted his satisfaction and spoke quietly.

'One of my lads was in earlier, Harry. Looking for a bloke with a bandaged hand.'

The attendant nodded vigorously.

'You've just missed him,' he said.

'Missed who?'

'The bloke with the hand.'

'Bloody hell!' Wilson frowned in disappointment. 'Don't tell me he's been and gone?'

'Not ten minutes ago. Hang on a bit.'

The attendant lowered his head to peer under the billiard-table shades till he found the wall-clock. 'No, a bit longer than that. I'd just made myself a brew. Half an hour, perhaps.'

'Well, did you find out who he was?'

'Yes and no.'

'Come on, Harry,' Wilson grumbled. 'What the hell do you mean by that?'

'He's the bloke you're after all right,' the attendant said, screwing his face into a broad wink. 'I'd swear to that.'

'Why?'

'It was written all over him, Mr Wilson. I can tell when a bloke's worried about something. And then there's the bandage and everything.'

'He did have a bandage then?'

'Just on one finger.' He demonstrated with his own digit. 'But like I told your mate, he had a bigger one on the day before, all over his hand.'

Henderson had said he was less than certain, but that sounded certain enough. Wilson liked the sound of it.

'Did you find out his name for us?' he asked.

'Not a chance. He wouldn't tell me a blind thing. In fact he got all steamed up

215

when I asked him things, specially when I said you chaps were looking for him.'

Wilson felt the cut of that, somewhere in his guts.

'Oh Christ! You shouldn't have told him that, Harry. Didn't young Henderson tell you to keep it quiet?'

The attendant registered the rebuke and was crestfallen. He began to mutter an apology but Wilson stopped him.

'Let it lie, Harry,' he said kindly. 'I don't suppose there's any harm done in the long run. Only I wish to God you hadn't told him.'

'I've got you a bit of something though,' the attendant said, his face brightening.

'Well, let's have it, then.'

The attendant pointed across the room.

'You see the bloke there on the corner table? Little chap with grey hair who's just cuing now?'

'What about him?'

'He knows the lad, that's what. He has a knock with him sometimes. I chatted him up when he came in.'

'Go on. What does he know about him?'

The attendant shrugged, pleased to shed the load of his involvement.

'You'd do better to ask him yourself,' he said. 'Watch out for him though. He hasn't a lot of love for you blokes.'

'I can manage without love,' Wilson said grimly. 'What I'm after is information.'

CHAPTER 18

So they were on to him. But how?

Nobody knew, so nobody could have talked. But maybe he was wrong about that? He had to be wrong somewhere, or they wouldn't be on his tail.

He knew damned well that he'd left no clues at any of his jobs, so he must have been recognised. Once he'd figured that out, he was sure he knew who'd seen his face and passed the word to the cops. Not the earlier ones, who'd all been frightened women. He'd always picked dark places anyway, and they couldn't have seen much of his face. And certainly not the one they were calling murder. Whether that girl knew him or not didn't matter, because she was dead. No, it had to be the last one—the blonde with the slippery mouth and the battering-ram knee.

And yet he'd had a close-up look at her both before and after, and he'd heard her voice spitting curses at him. If he'd known the girl—even vaguely—he'd have realised it then. And she couldn't have picked him out from those photograph books that the bobbies always used, because he wasn't in any books. That was the beauty of it. The cops knew nothing at all about him—or hadn't, until now.

It must have something to do with those running feet.

Somebody had chased him that day and he'd been so worked up at the time that he'd never even got a look at who it was. But the other bloke might have known him? Oh yes. That wasn't as long a shot as it seemed.

He was no stranger in the district, after all. He'd spent all his life in Cotteston and he'd gone to school with hundreds of other kids from round and about the town. Not only kids, either. Hundreds of youths as well, during the one year when his old man had insisted on him going to night classes to improve his education. Thank God, the old man had croaked at the end of that year, and his mother, weak, watery bitch, had only made mild clucking noises when he ducked classes for ever.

Or what about his workmates?

He'd never held down much in the way of a job, but there'd been a couple of short stints in local factories and a longer one as a general gad-about at Cotteston Market Hall. The list of people who might remember him from there was bloody endless. And then there was the cinemas, the discos and the gathererd crowds at week-end football matches. He didn't bother with such things nowadays, but he'd been keen enough up to six months ago. Oh yes, he'd been around, and his face was certain to be known to a lot of people in Cotteston.

But the first place they'd gone looking for him was the billiard hall. Not the discos or the Market or anywhere like that. So was the billiard hall the place where somebody had clocked him? And was it somebody from the billiard hall who'd come upon him tackling the blonde and passed on a memory of his face to those bastards at the nick? What a pity he hadn't checked on the owner of those running feet, because if he'd had the presence of mind to take a sight of the bloke he might not be so worried now. Might not have to wonder about who'd put the squeak in.

Well, that was one vital lesson he'd learned. His face was too well known, and even in the early mornings there might be somebody about who'd recognise it. It had happened once already, so there was nothing to stop it happening again.

Unless he did something about it? Unless he made bloody sure from now on that nobody *could* see his face?

The idea pleased him. There must be plenty of ways he could cover up. He needed a mask of some sort. Something that wouldn't get in the way, but would cover him up all the time so that nobody could possibly recognise him. He'd give it some thought and have a good scheme ready for next time.

Because there had to be a next time.

He wasn't going to be put off just because the jacks had started asking questions. He'd give up snooker for a while, he'd have to do that, but he wasn't going to give up this special brand of hunting that never failed to satisfy his feelings. Up to press he hadn't had the best of luck, but luck was something that could change. He'd just need to be more careful, that was all. Besides, there were failures and failures. He'd collected a few nasty knocks to his hide, but he'd never failed yet to grab hold of a woman, feel her against him, come out of the encounter satisfied to a degree.

The fact that the jacks had started to get nosy only meant that he'd have to lay off for a bit—let things die down before he made another move. And there was no hurry. He had all the time in the world. He'd give it a day or two, a week, perhaps, and then hit 'em again in a way they wouldn't be expecting.

★ ★ ★ ★

He was very tempted to lie doggo, because he knew the risks of moving too soon. But he still felt the fever in his blood. If anything, it was keener than ever and he couldn't possibly disregard it for long.

After two days he was itching to try again.

★ ★ ★ ★

Wilson was disappointed with what had seemed a promising lead. He soft-talked the snooker-player for all he was worth and didn't ease off till his persistence looked like ruining the game. But the outcome was scarcely worth his time.

'It's next door to hopeless, sir,' he said dolefully as he was relating his discoveries to Detective Chief Superintendent Evans. 'A first name that's as common as muck and a street with about a thousand bloody houses. We'd be at it for ages sorting that lot out.'

'If we look hard enough, we'll find him,' Evans said.

'Oh, we'll find him all right in the end, if we have to turn over every bloody house in the street. But I ask you. Wouldn't you think somebody would know him a bit better?'

The door opened to admit Detective Superintendent Challon and Detective Sergeant Hollis. Evans nodded a greeting.

'You'd better go back to the beginning, Jim,' he suggested. 'See what these two can make of it.'

'He's a big powerful lad evidently,' Wilson said, 'but not all that old—twenty at the most. He's been using Harry Kilner's place for six months or so, nearly every afternoon. He was definitely in there two days ago with a bandage on his hand. Then, this afternoon, he turned up there again. The big bandage was missing but he had a smaller one round his little finger.' He paused and looked round at his colleagues. 'So when our young lady says she bit his finger, she was spot on. If nothing else, we've a fair idea of the bloke we're looking for.'

'What's his name?' Challon asked hopefully.

'Joe.'

'Joe what?' Challon looked bemused.

'Just Joe, sir. No second name. That's the bugger of it. I found this chap who knows him, but he doesn't know him well enough. His first name and not a damned thing more. Except where he thinks he lives.'

'All right then—where does he live?'

'Rosamund Street.'

'What number?'

'No number. Just a street.'

'Oh hell,' Challon was clearly disgusted. 'Half the bloody town lives there, Jim. It's the longest street in these parts. The builders got sloshed and forgot when to stop. There's houses down both sides and deadlegs living ten to a house in damned near every one.'

'I know that,' Wilson said with feeling. 'Like I was just telling the boss, we'd need a Task Force for a fortnight to sort that place properly.'

'What about the burgess list?' Challon said. 'I know we've only got one name, but we could eliminate a lot of folk who are called something different.'

'I've already had a run through,' Wilson said. 'I've found nineteen Josephs, and that's only the adults, remember. Chances are this kid isn't old enough yet to be registered as a voter, so he could be from any single house in the entire street. And bear in mind, my informant isn't sure about it. He only *thinks* he lives there.'

Evans sounded a more hopeful note.

'I still say it's a break-through,' he pointed out. 'Until Jim picked up this lead he might have been anybody at all and lived anywhere. We've got close on a hundred thousand souls in Cotteston, and till now there was nothing to say he lived in Cotteston at all. It wouldn't be the first time we'd had a Manchester bloke operating on our patch. Now though, if the gen's good, we've got it down to a single street. A bloody long street, perhaps, but it makes the odds a lot more favourable. And we've got a name—just a first name—but that'll give us a good lift. The thing is, how do we set about finding him?'

'I can think of three ways straight off,' Challon offered. 'We know he used · the billiard hall, so that's number one. Number two is Council records—the register of births—to sort out all the Joes we've had wished on us in the right age group. A long job, maybe, but we've got plenty of staff to spread the load.'

'And number three?' Evans prompted.

'The old method. We go knocking on doors.'

But Wilson had yet to deliver his final blow.

'I'm all for the second and third,' he said, 'but as far as the first goes, we've had it. You can bet your life this bloke won't be playing snooker for a while.'

'How's that, Jim?' Challon asked.

'Because he knows we're after him. That silly bugger Harry Kilner told him so, in spite of young Henderson warning him not to.'

'He deserves to be criticized with a foot up his backside,' Evans scowled.

Wilson grinned at the empty, fanciful threat.

'We can't fall out with Harry, sir,' he said, 'because he was only doing his bit for us. It seems he pumped the lad a bit too obviously and got his back right up. Then, when the lad challenged him, he blurted out that one of our blokes had been in there asking questions. That's all he said, and then he tried to pass it off. But he must have well and truly wised the lad up. I'll gamble he doesn't go snookering for a bit.'

'I wonder how scared he is?' Challon said. 'If he's only gone to ground we might still trace him by canvassing Rosamund Street. But suppose he's got the wind up properly? He might have decided to move out—and that would make the job a real stumour.'

'He won't know how much we know, Ralph,' Evans said.

'No. And that helps us a bit. The chances are he'll just skulk at home where we can lay our hands on him.'

Matt Hollis had been a listener until now. Now he voiced a suggestion.

'We could always stake the place out, sir.'

As always Evans was prepared to listen to anything. 'All right, Matt. What's on your mind?'

'Well, we know what time he operates, don't we? And he's been very persistent so far. He killed one girl, which should have been enough to turn anybody off, but it didn't turn this bloke off. A couple of days later, he's having another go. I think we should use his persistence. There might be a bit of risk involved, but I vote we set our stall out to catch him on the job.'

'How the hell can we do that, Matt? He can strike anywhere he likes. We'd need a thousand men.'

'We wait for him leaving home, sir. That's not as difficult as it sounds. There aren't many ways out of Rosamund Street when you think about it. With about four men stationed in the right places we could cut off everybody who moves out of the street. If we do that from the time the early buses start running, we might get lucky. And we wouldn't have to wait till he attacked somebody. All we'd have to do would be check people's hands. With the description we've got, plus that hand, we could pluck him like a flower.'

They waited patiently—heard him out—and then Evans was conscious of all eyes centring on him. It was his decision and they waiting for it.

'It's worth a try,' he said. 'The checking of records is a must, and we'll get some men on that right away. But as for knocking on doors in Rosamund Street, I'd prefer to leave that till we've given Matt's idea a run. We'll do it for the next few days at any rate. We'll be on the job bright and early to see if this Joe shows himself.'

'And if he doesn't?' Challon said.

'If he doesn't show, Ralph, we'll pull in every man we've got and go through Rosamund Street like a dose of salts. But we watch first. So get some shifts worked out, Ralph, and we'll agree on the best places to stake out. Use our own lads as far as we can, but if you need more, have a word with Henry Naylor and get some of his uniform lads to mix in.'

He paused and surveyed the gathering.

'And no slip ups, lads,' he finished. 'We've got to catch this bugger before some other woman gets a nasty ride.'

CHAPTER 19

It was a still, chilly morning with a hint of mist swirling round the street lamps. From his hiding place, Detective Constable Laurie Flood stared glumly out on the unappealing vista and yawned expansively.

He could hardly keep his eyes open.

It was entirely his own fault, and he knew it. He'd had the previous evening off and he'd been given plenty of advance warning that today would be an early stint. Jenny was on early duty too, but she'd shown a bit more cokum. She'd insisted on leaving the club half-way through the cabaret and, reluctantly, he'd dropped her off at home by eleven.

Jenny had turned-in early and there'd been nothing in the world to stop Flood doing the same. But instead he'd moved on to a couple of places he knew, swilled dirty ale all night and crawled into bed in the small hours. Having to start work at half-past-five was bad enough in all conscience, but doing so after less than three hours of uneasy sleep, punctuated by bladder-easing trips to the bathroom, had left him feeling shattered and wrung out.

This was the second morning of obboes, but thank God he'd missed the first. It had been a complete waste of time, as these watching jobs so often were. Today would probably be a repeat performance he told himself darkly. Not that the task dismayed him. Indeed, Flood had more than once struck lucky in the same sort of circumstances. The countless hours he'd spent in the past, watching for some event or other that never came about, were more than compensated for by those few occasions when his efforts had paid off.

It was cold in the shrubbery, cold and damp, and the rustling fronds of rhododendron touched clammy against his neck. But the vantage was a good one. In an untrodden patch like that there was no risk whatever of being seen by curious people, especially at that early hour. And by staring through a gap in the foliage he could see the whole area of the north end of Rosamund Street. Somewhere along there in the vast stretch of dark terraced houses was the man Flood had been appointed to look for, and he knew what was expected of him if the man showed.

There were four other colleagues sharing the task.

D.C Phil Meecham had been allotted the south end, and the other three were spaced out at intervals along the street in the best cover they could find. So it was a lottery. Either the quarry appeared or he didn't, and if he did appear, Flood had a five-to-one chance of being the one to spot him. It was only a matter of waiting and using his eyes.

Flood had sorted out a dry patch for his backside—or a patch that had seemed dry. Now he could feel the dampness striking up from the soil and gradually seeping into the seat of his trousers. Any minute now he'd have to change position, rise to his haunches and prop his cramped body squarely on his feet. Not for a few more minutes though. He huddled into the folds of his overcoat, screwed his eyes against the onset of sleep and struggled to concentrate.

The happening developed in an unforeseen way.

One minute Flood was staring out on a deserted scene and the next he found himself looking directly at the dark silhouette of a man. When first seen, the man was standing quite still on the pavement across the far side of the carriageway, directly opposite Flood's hiding place.

How had he arrived there? Flood had to admit that he hadn't the slightest idea. And that was a devil of a problem. Because if the man had emerged from Rosamund Street he might easily be Flood's target. But suppose he hadn't? There were a number of other streets converging on this point and the bloke could have come out of any one of them.

Flood cursed his unrealised moment of inattention.

It was bloody marvellous how you could watch like mad for ages and then when you blinked your eyes for a minute, the thing you'd been waiting for happened unseen. He checked his watch. Ten past six. Well, the time was right, so this could easily be the bloke. There was nothing for it but to get up, cross over to the man and go through the motions of checking him—particularly his hands. With a little bit of luck he'd turn out to be the right man, and Flood's aching stint of crouching in the bushes would be at an end.

On the other hand, suppose he turned out to be some innocent shift-worker on his way to or from work? Well, it would take only a few minutes to find that out, and then he could return to the shrubbery and continue watching.

Before Flood could move, the man moved.

He seemed to turn on a sudden impulse and within half a minute he was moving away. Away from Rosamund Street.

This was the kind of dilemma that Flood could well have done without. To check the man now, he'd have to follow him, catch him up and ask questions. But to belt after him full tilt would put him on his guard, and if he turned out to be the right man that might mean losing him, especially if—as it certainly appeared—he was a young, athletic type. Worst of all, it meant that Flood would have to leave his post, and he could imagine the criticism that would shower on his head if he followed a decoy and lost the real bird.

For a delaying few seconds, Flood thought he might ignore the bloke—let him walk away as though he'd never even seen him—but at heart Flood was not that kind of coward. He emerged from the shrubbery and stood blinking after the departing figure. At least two hundred yards separated them by this time, and it would take a bit of hurrying to make up the leeway. But it would have to be done. Flood set off after the man, moving with ever-lengthening strides.

The gap between them seemed to be closing far too slowly, yet Flood was striding out so obviously by now that if the bloke looked back it would be a dead give-away. So far, he hadn't looked back, but the risk was always there. Yet if Flood slowed his pace too much the gap might start to widen and he couldn't risk losing the man altogether.

To hell with it! Flood decided. In this job you had to be a bit of a gambler, and even at the expense of maybe spoiling the job he'd pin his hopes on a good roll of the dice. Having come so far, he'd lost his grip on Rosamund Street anyway, and even if he went back he could never be sure he hadn't missed out. So he'd have to bank on the dark figure moving ahead of him proving to be the bloke he was after. He slowed his speed slightly and began to trail rather than overtake.

The man moved purposefully ahead till he came to the first wide junction on his left. Langford Lane! He stopped at the junction and seemed undecided which route to take, looking first along the road ahead and then left along the wide lane. Flood found a handy privet hedge and ducked into its shadows, waiting there with his heart pounding in this throat. The man turned left into Langford Lane and disappeared from Flood's sight.

Somehow, Flood picked up a message from what he'd seen and a tiny thrill insinuated itself into his mind. He felt lucky. He knew this was going to be the right bloke. Langford Lane was one of the main bus routes into town. Not one where they'd had any attacks reported so far, but as recent events had shown, the attacker was beginning to move about a bit, breaking fresh ground. He slipped from behind the bush, walked quickly to the junction and took a cautious peep round the corner.

His heart nearly stopped completely.

The man was no more than ten yards away, standing next to a garden wall with his head cocked in a listening posture. Flood drew his head back and waited, hardly daring to breathe. Had the bastard heard something and grown suspicious? Flood was light-footed by nature and was wearing soft-soled shoes, so it wasn't likely that his footfalls would have carried that far. Besides, the bloke wouldn't have waited there if he'd sensed he was being followed.

After a dragging interval he risked another cautious peep. The man had moved on again and was fifty yards away along the lane. He was moving slowly, his head swinging perceptibly from side to side as he went.

Flood grinned his appreciation. The bugger was looking ahead to check bus stops. He'd started to hunt.

It occurred to Flood that he might have missed another trick. He could easily have nipped round the corner, faced the man and checked him out in accordance with the drill. But the time for that was past, and in any case it seemed more appropriate to wait and watch. But traipsing after him on a one-to-one basis might not be the best way to handle it. There were others on duty besides Laurie Flood and a spot of assistance wouldn't come amiss. He took out his personal radio and hefted it speculatively. Yes. That might be the best thing to do.

Wally Grinton was on Station-duty. His voice came through quite clearly in response to Flood's call, but as usual, he sounded crusty.

'Speak up, caller. I can't hear a bloody word.'

'It's Laurie Flood, Wally you great twit,' he said, raising his voice slightly above a whisper. 'I can't speak any louder. The bugger's near enough to listen in.'

★ ★ ★ ★

Matt Hollis received the relayed message within seconds. He was patrolling the outskirts of the town at the wheel of the C.I.D runabout and he was tuned in for just such a call. Jenny Collinge, wearing plain clothes for the occasion, was in the front passenger seat.

'Got it, Wally,' Hollis acknowledged, 'and we're right next door to Langford Lane. We'll be there in a couple of minutes.'

'Need any help, Sarge?'

'No thanks, Wally. Not close-up stuff anyway—that might spoil things. But you can get some cars in position a bit further out. If we happen to miss him I'll get through to you and they can cordon the area off.'

Hollis gunned the engine of the little Ford, knowing exactly the route to follow. If there was one advantage in policing the same town for a lot of years it lay in knowledge of the area. Every nook and cranny in Cotteston was listed in Matt Hollis' mind and the main roads were an open book to him.

The old excitement was coursing in Hollis, but Jenny Collinge was more overtly thrilled than he. The years of her service were beginning to tot up, but comparatively she was still green and to be involved in an up-to-the-minute chase like this was a rare experience.

'Do we watch to see what he does, Sarge, or do we just grab him?' Jenny wanted to know.

The plot of events was already hatching in Hollis' mind.

'We do neither, Jenny,' he said. 'That's if you're prepared to play it the way I want it played.'

'How's that, Sarge?' she asked him curiously.

'I reckon we'll go fishing,' he told her. 'In less than a minute we'll be at the top end of Langford Lane and the lad we're after should be half-way along—let's say a quarter of a mile from us. He's looking for a woman at a bus stop. You're a woman, Jenny, and a damned attractive one.' He stopped and gave her an obvious leer. 'So all we need is a bus stop and we can set the stage, and there are scods of bus stops in Langford Lane. Are you game to try?'

'Let him attack me, you mean?'

'Yes, if necessary. But you needn't worry about that, Jenny, because I'll be skulking about.'

'Can I defend myself?'

He heard the words, but he also noted the way she said them. There was no sign of worry or indecision in her tones. She was grinning broadly.

'You can kick him where it hurts,' he said with an answering grin, 'and if you don't know where that is, I'd be happy to tell you.'

'Don't tempt me, Sergeant,' she said.

CHAPTER 20

Hollis drove fast towards the rendevous.

The last lap lay along a dimly lighted side street bordered by open land on one side and by a school on the other. Directly ahead they could see the broader, brighter strip of light that was Langford Lane. He stopped the car a few yards short of the junction, reached over and gave her shoulder a reassuring squeeze as she climbed out.

Jenny's legs were shaking as she moved from comparative darkness to brave the sodium lights of Langford Lane. She hoped the tremble wasn't a sign of cowardice—convinced herself that it couldn't be—hoped also that the sergeant wouldn't notice.

But there was a certain strain about the situation that couldn't be ignored. A great deal might easily depend on the little acting role Sergeant Hollis had given her. She badly wanted the trap to work and there was the uncomfortable feeling that if it didn't work, she'd be the one to have bungled it. To let the side down like that would be quite unforgivable, and Jenny felt the shame of that possibility, even before it happened.

At the first stop there was nobody waiting, and when she neared it she slowed almost to a stop. But then, looking diagonally across the wide carriageway, she could just make out the opposing stop a hundred or more yards away—and waiting at it was a woman. She was a young and attractive woman it seemed. Jenny's heart dropped to her blue wedge-heels.

Blast the silly woman, whoever she was.

With a target like that standing between, her man would never get this far. He'd either attack the other woman or—more likely—be put off by her own presence and sheer away from both of them. The thought occurred to her that the charade need no longer be played through—that they could simply use this other woman as bait in the way Jenny herself was to have been used—but strong within her she could feel the rumblings of professional pride. Having been set the task, she was unable to accept the idea of ducking out in favour of some other unsuspecting victim.

Damn the woman again for a nuisance. By just being there, she was likely to spoil everything.

Looking beyond the woman into the misty channel of light she could see no other people about, and it occurred to Jenny that the thing might still work if she moved further along the lane. It was worth trying. Reaching a decision she moved quickly, click-clicking along the broad pavement, past the waiting woman and on to the next bus stop.

It was empty—and so was the road at that point.

Jenny leaned against the stop, fumbled in the depths of her handbag, produced a handkerchief and lightly blew her nose. Then she settled her eyes in a vacant stare on the houses opposite—and waited.

The man seemed to spring up from no where.

When she first became aware of him, he was fifteen yards away, and closing. Unbidden, her heart commenced to thump in a beat that must surely be audible. From the corner of her eye she watched his approach, wanting all the time to turn and face him, to confront the man and dare him to come any closer. But she knew that was not the way.

To stand unmoving, pretending not to see, called for a massive effort of will, but Jenny managed it. The man's progress over the intervening flagstones seemed to take an age, and in the last few seconds she could no longer see anything, because the man had moved out of her vision and was standing directly behind her.

The short hairs on her neck bristled as she sensed him closing in. There was a faint scuffing noise that might have been anything but still the attack didn't come. Even now, the whole thing might be a mistake. There was no law against a man waiting for a bus, and just because a woman stood waiting at the same stop, that didn't put it out of bounds. He might be just an innocent...

There was a sudden white blur as an object fell downwards in front of her eyes and then a choking, stifling sensation as something tightened about her neck. At the same time a body pressed hard against hers and she could hear the man grunting and panting as he twisted...twisted...

The moment had arrived to fight, but it was impossible to fight. Jenny could neither scream nor struggle. The ligature about her neck was like a steel band constricting her windpipe. She was able to exhale once—and to partly refill her straining lungs, but then the blockage became absolute and she could only strive to hold on to her senses as she felt her body being dragged obliquely away, trailing behind the man like a bolt of cloth, her lax heels scraping along the road's asphalt surface.

★ ★ ★ ★

Matt Hollis came nearer to making a tragic blunder than at any other time in his service.

He'd picked his spot with care. He could see Jenny's trim figure as she moved towards the empty bus stop and before she reached it he was in position, eighty yards behind her, standing in a gateway where he blended with the privet hedge.

Unable, at that distance, to see the other woman at the opposing stop, he was taken completely off guard when he saw Jenny hesitate and then walk on. What the bloody hell was the girl playing at? They'd agreed the stop in advance, but now for some unknown reason, she'd changed the plan. He had no idea why, and it was impossible to ask her, so he could only move from his own position and tag along behind.

But that sort of manoeuvre had to be done carefully. He flitted his heavy frame from gate to gate along the front of the mercifully unlighted houses, making as much speed as he dared. But he was gradually falling behind.

He could see Jenny all the time, and that was comforting, but by the time she reached the next stop and stood leaning against it the gap between them was uncomfortably large. He continued to edge slowly towards her, using every bit of cover he could find. And when, some distance beyond Jenny, he saw the approaching figure of a man, he slowed in an agony of indecision.

The speed and ferocity of the attack terrified him.

A mere second before it happened, he'd seen the man standing close behind Jenny, fumbling in his pockets and playing with some object, but at that distance he could make out no detail. Then, when the man made his move, it was too late to do anything but run.

Desperately, Hollis abandoned stealth and ran as fast as he could go, but the distance to the scene was alarmingly great and there was panic underlying his breathlessness. He saw the man begin to drag Jenny away, trundling her across the carriageway, obviously heading for a dark gap between houses on the opposite side. And fifty enormous yards still lay between. The scene was unreal, terrifying, and Hollis began to sweat with fear as he realised he might be very much too late.

But he worried without cause.

Beyond the attacker and his unresisting burden another figure appeared, moving like a whippet on a converging course. Hollis recognised the lanky, shock-headed, welcome figure of young Laurie Flood and he almost wept with relief. By the time Matt Hollis arrived, the attacker was a helpless prisoner in Flood's hands, held by the throat and pinned against the brickwork of a garden wall.

But Hollis had no thought for anyone except Jenny.

Ignoring Flood and the prisoner, he ran straight to the girl, lying still and silent on a patch of rank grass bordering the pavement, a white silk scarf pulled tight about her neck. In an agony of fright he snatched the ends of the scarf and rapidly unwound the ligature. He was at once rewarded by a rising of her chest and the gasp of air rushing into her throat. It was the most gratifying sound he'd heard in many a long day and he responded vocally, cloaking his joy in blasphemy as men are inclined to do.

'Thank Christ! Oh thank bloody Christ!'

* * * *

Within seconds Jenny was stirring and breathing more easily. Leaving her then, Hollis went to Flood and tapped him on the shoulder. He looked beyond Flood, and for the first time since the series of crimes had started he looked on the face of the attacker.

Except that it was not a face at all.

It was a mask—literally a mask—the moulder rubber features of a puck, a harlequin. Hollis reached out and snatched the rubber shell away revealing the scowling, snarling face beneath. It was an ordinary face, but running with sweat and twisted into a look of hate.

'Let's have the cuffs on, Laurie,' he

snapped. 'Then I'll hold him while you help Jenny to the car.'

'Help who?' Flood seemed flabbergasted.

'Jenny Collinge. Who did you think it was?'

Flood looked sideways at the girl, recognising her for the first time, and a surge of anger welled in him. Tightening his grip on the prisoner's throat he balled his fist and raised it high.

'I'll kill him,' he shouted. 'I'll beat his bloody brains in.'

But Matt Holllis fended the blow.

'Save it, Laurie,' he said. 'The bastard isn't worth the trouble. Before we're through with him you'll have all the satisfaction you want. Now leave him to me and go and help Jenny, like I said.'

CHAPTER 21

Rosemary Sanderson had come to Cotteston Pollice Station timidly, filled with pinpricks of dread.

The message, delivered verbally at her home by a young constable, had been plain enough. Would she please call in at some convenient time to speak to Sergeant Hollis about her handbag?

Well, she'd arrived, and the sergeant had given her the bag. Not that she'd ever be able to use it again. The strap was broken, the clasp dull, the bag itself badly scratched and covered with mud and slime. But it was her bag.

Oh yes, it's mine,' she said in answer to his query. 'Where did you get it?'

'He'd stowed it in a culvert down near the river. It's a wonder nobody's found it before now.'

'Who found it?'

'I did. But I knew where to look. Between you and me, Miss Sanderson, we've got the lad in custody. I can't tell you anything more than that, because he has to come before court on serious charges, but he told me where he'd hidden the bag, so I collected it.'

'Are the things still inside?'

'Some of them. Not the money, I'm afraid. He's spent that. I'd like you to check the contents and tell me if there's anything missing besides the money.'

Rosemary opened the bag and riffled cursorily through the contents. She was looking for a white envelope and the other things meant nothing. But there was no envelope. Hollis could see the dismay clouding her face.

'It isn't there,' she wailed.

He opened a drawer, took out an envelope and held it out to her.

'Is this what you're looking for?'

'Oh yes.' Her face brightened.

'I'd like you to make sure it's the same,' he said.

She slipped the letter from the envelope —examined it.

'Yes. It's the one I told you about.'

'I rather thought so. All right, Miss Sanderson, now listen to me. I kept that letter separate for obvious reasons. I've listed the contents of your handbag in our receipts book and I haven't included the letter. I haven't even read it, if you'd like to know. What I want you to do is sign for the bag and contents, all except the letter. Is that fair enough?'

'And the letter?' she said with trembling lip.

'I'd burn it if I were you. In fact, I've a box of matches here and I'd be happy to do it for you. Shall I?'

She nodded—speechless.

250

He fired the letter—held its corner between thumb and finger and steered the flames until nothing remained but black ash. He dropped the ash into a litter bin, stirred it with a desk-ruler until it was as fine as dust.

'And now,' he said, 'I'd forget it ever existed.'

★ ★ ★ ★

Jenny was much too dignified to crow in public, but privately she rejoiced in the happenings of the day.

It was some time before her bruised throat ceased to pain her, but the good things, the glory and acclaim, the sense of achievement, and most of all the startling improvement in her relationship with Laurie Flood, all combined to bolster her ego in a delightful way.

The prisoner she knew, had admitted everything.

There was still a possibility that the charge of murder would be reduced to manslaughter at the hearing, but that was a matter for authorities higher than Jenny. There would in any case, be a number of other serious charges, including one of attempted murder in respect of the attack on herself.

And now, to add shine to the event, there'd been a marvellously worded letter signed by the Chief Constable. Jenny could almost remember the letter verbatim, but what it meant was that whenever anybody examined her personal record from that time on, they'd find the words, 'HIGHLY COMMENDED'.

But it was the social benefit that pleased Jenny most.

Ever since the event, Laurie Flood had shown an almost insatiable interest in her and every free evening for a long time to come was booked as a date with Laurie.

Not only that, but the quality of his attention had improved too. Before this, she'd been a challenge to him, to be conquered if possible, but now he'd blossomed into a much nicer person than she'd given him credit for being. All of a sudden, his ambitions had taken a less predatory direction and it seemed rosily possible that before very long...

But she'd handle that moment when it came.

In the meantime it was three o'clock on a cold morning and she'd just crawled into bed after a late night out and a controlled snogging session on the doorstep. She felt physically tired, but that was all to the good, because there were seven long hours of sleep between now and when she had to turn out on duty again.

Snuggling into the sheets, she ignored the rattle of gravel against the window, but when handful followed handful she could ignore it no longer. She struggled out of bed, crossed to the window, opened it and peered out. There was a panda car parked outside, and the uniformed figure standing on the lawn, in the act of bending for more gravel, was unmistakably Frank Johnson.

'Go away, Frank,' she grumbled. 'It's night time.'

'Night time or not, you're wanted, Jenny.'

'Oh Lord! Not again. What is it this time?'

'A drunken driver.'

'Come off it, Frank. I don't deal with drunken drivers.'

He grinned apologetically.

'You'll have to come and deal with this one, Jenny. 'It's a roaring, swearing, drunken *woman* driver.'

The publishers hope that this book has given you enjoyable reading. Large Print Books are especially designed to be as easy to see and hold as possible. If you wish a complete list of our books, please ask at your local library or write directly to: Dales Large Print, Long Preston, North Yorkshire, BD23 4ND England.